KAT DRUMMOND BOOK THREE

DEVIL'S GAMBIT

NICHOLAS WOODE-SMITH

Copyright © 2019

Kat Drummond

ISBN: 9781698260549

Contents

Chapter 1. Fire

Don't play with fire.

Simple lesson, but simple lessons are often the most important. Too bad I wasn't following it myself. Well, give someone enough money and they'll cuddle with a salamander. Lucky for me, I was just being paid to kill it.

Still, that last streak of fire, shot out like llama spit, was a bit too close for comfort. This wasn't my usual type of job. I'm an undead hunter. I specialise in exterminating the rotting and reanimated and those who brought them back. Had put down more zombies than I could count and even a human necromancer who had insisted on bringing the dead back to life. Had almost been arrested for that – but was let off. Killing monsters was my profession and humans are often the biggest monsters.

Even with my specialty, I'd been very much out of my comfort zone recently. Exorcising ghosts, hunting vampires and tracking down filing cabinets with teeth. But even with such diversification, this salamander was still completely outside of my expertise. But a job was a job. And I always get the job done.

I just hoped this particular job wouldn't burn me to cinders.

"Get behind it," Treth, the incorporeal and otherworldly knight living in my head, ordered. He sounded inappropriately calm given the situation. We'd been in plenty of fights before, but never with this much fire. It wasn't helping that my monster hunter get-up involved a sweltering bite-resistant thick scarf and a padded leather jacket.

I peeked around the corner of a very flammable white wall in a suburban house. A currently burning suburban house, I might add. A gust of flames almost hit me as I pulled back.

"Easier said than done, Treth," I hissed through gritted teeth. The hilts of my recently repaired swords were getting hot. Made it worse that I was clutching them with enough force to crush an ogre's handshake. It was even hotter underneath my mask. Was still better than my old one. I had to dump my old black and white polymer mask after a run-in with a vampire cartel that had abducted my friend, Trudie. My efforts to save her were not exactly legal and some vampires had enough public sympathy to start a manhunt for a person with my type of mask. The hunt was also the reason my swords had to be repaired. Usually, I'd buy some new blades, but these guys deserved a bit of care. They'd gone through a lot and earned me a fair amount of money. Even so, that altercation with the vampires had taught me their limitations.

My new mask was more than an adequate replacement for the old. My friend, Pranish, a skilled wizard, had enchanted a metal face plate to be my new mask. He had made it translucent on one side, while solid on the other,allowing me to remain anonymous without sacrificing my peripheral vision. It was also a lot stronger than my old get-up. A zombie had broken its hand attempting to punch my face a few days back. I'd almost burst out laughing. Treth sent me his voiceless displeasure at my reaction, but I also sensed some amusement from him. We both hated the undead. Regardless of all our other differences, that simple thing kept us on the same path.

Even with Pranish's face plate, I'm not sure my face would survive a full fire blast from a salamander, though. Not much would.

I risked a glance at the creature. It was perched on top of a tiled kitchen countertop, hissing up a storm and salivating lava. It smelled like burnt popcorn and charcoal. On the face of it, it wasn't nearly as ugly as my usual fare. I hunted rotting corpses for a living, after all. Couldn't get much worse than that. This creature just looked like an orange, enflamed lizard. Just, it was only the size of a Great Dane. Not exactly ugly, but not kitten-cute either.

My fixer, Conrad Khoi, had brought me on the case just before I was going to go running in myself. Had smelled the burning from my apartment and I wasn't a fan of some rift-made monster setting my neighbourhood on fire. Don't get me wrong. Wasn't doing it out of the altruistic goodness of my heart. I just don't want monsters lowering the property values of my neighbourhood.

But, I rent...

And if the property values go down, the rent will go down...

Why am I helping again?

Ah, yes. It's my job. Forgot. Well, at least I'll get paid. But as was often the case with my profession, I now wondered if any pay day was worth it.

Running in was a bad idea, I now realised. I wasn't equipped to fight a salamander. My clothing was flammable, very much so. Can you blame me? Not many people own flame-retardant outfits. Lucky for me, this salamander was small for its size. A juvenile. While it had already immolated the lounge's couch, armchair, rug and part of its flat screen TV, it was struggling to set the walls alight. Hope City houses were a disparate mix of wood and brick and, while this house had plenty of wooden interior walls, it also had plenty of brick. So, I was still alive. Alive enough to hear Treth complain.

"This isn't our type of fight, Kat."

I opened my mouth to reply but, instead, dodged as a golf ball-sized sphere of fire exploded where I had been standing moments before.

"Ours is the type of fight that pays, Treth," I replied, eying possible angles of attack.

I felt him roll his eyes. I never saw his gestures or expressions, but always felt them, like some wordless inclination. Treth could see my body language, so it was only fair. Well, not completely. I didn't know what he looked like. Knew very little about him except that he'd come to Earth from a medieval world after being killed by his lich brother. While I didn't like that my family was dead, at least they weren't undead. Some consolation.

The salamander stopped its tirade of fire and scuttled off the counter, around the corner and out of my sight.

"What's the blighter doing now?"

"Wouldn't be having to think so hard if we were purging the undead."

I rolled my eyes this time. Treth and I both hated the undead, but we were both monster hunters first. But Treth always made undead hunting a higher priority on the monster hunting menu. I'd tend to agree, seeing as my parents had been killed by undead and necromancers, but I also needed to eat. Undead just weren't paying as much in bounties these days.

I used to be a bit squeamish about killing non-undead, but after killing a human necromancer and then swathes of sentient vampires, I'd lost a bit of respect for the sanctity of life. And undead or not, this salamander was a monster. And as I will remind you a lot: I slay monsters.

"Well, go after it," Treth said with irritated resignation.

"Why so grumpy today?" I asked, proceeding forward in a combat stance, ready to use my dual swords violently and efficiently if the salamander doubled back on me.

"I don't like the heat and I don't like distractions from the crusade."

Treth's crusade/destiny/quest was a vague goal of eliminating the endless hordes of undead and evil creatures that now infested Earth and the other planes. In general, I agreed with him about it, but I was also a tad less idealistic, or specific, about what I should kill.

"This salamander's a monster, Treth."

"Not like an undead."

"It is burning these people's house down."

I peeked around the corner down a hallway. Flaming claw-prints marked the way, veering around a juncture at the end of the hall. I stepped over the tracks carefully, as every track spat fire inches high. Didn't want to damage my new boots. Yet, at least.

"Can't blame it. It is in its nature. It cannot not burn things."

"A salamander expert now?" I chided. "And isn't it the nature of the zombie to consume? Why not give it amnesty?"

That shut him up.

I reached the end of the hallway. No sign of the salamander, but definite signs of its passing. The cream carpet was pockmarked with scorched clawed footprints, dotted with little tiny flames. Just to add insult to injury, the creature had also scratched metre long slashes into the walls, right through some paintings.

"Such vandalism! Such chaos! I'd say this creature is evil, Treth," I said, imitating his lecture voice and then grinning. I'd been grinning in life-threatening situations a lot more lately. A coping mechanism or oncoming insanity, I'm not sure. I'm just glad Trudie wasn't here to see it. Would definitely double her nagging.

The molten tracks stopped at a shattered glass sliding door. The rubber between the frame and the glass was bubbling. I frowned. I hoped that my swords would be okay. Steel didn't melt that easily, but they could still be scorched. Extreme heat wasn't that good for most things.

The creature had gone outside, into the grassy backyard. Instead of disparate flaming footprints, a trail of fire led directly up to it, as it looked right at me and shot a fireball the size of a microwave. It probably expected me to run away at the display. I don't run away.

I dove under the flaming projectile, rolled and jumped back onto my feet. The salamander was shocked for a second, and then ran, setting fire to a lavender bush. It was a cowardly little bastard, thankfully. I had only caught a glance of its claws, but they looked as long as steak knives. I'm glad he didn't feel confident enough to use them. Well, to be fair, my swords were longer.

"Kat, he's running circles around us. He's going to surround us in flames."

Nonsense, he's just retreating…

Oh, wait.

A wall of flame wreathed a scorched circle around us, radiating heat. I was struggling to find my breath.

Well, drat.

"Any smart ideas? Something other than we should have gone hunting wights."

"Never fought a salamander, Kat."

Of course, he hadn't. Salamanders weren't from his world or mine. They came to Earth through rifts – portals from different worlds.

"But," he continued. "If a salamander is fiery, then it must hate water."

"So, I throw a glass of water at it?"

I felt Treth's glare.

The salamander had stopped to examine its handiwork, as I was pinned by a waist high wall of flame. Just behind it was the house.

This must have been a nice garden before the salamander got to it. My landlady, Mrs Ndlovu, also had a nice garden. She watered it constantly.

I grinned.

"Brace yourself, Treth," I said, needlessly. He was a spirit. He couldn't be hurt himself. Only felt a bit of what I felt.

"What are…"

He stopped speaking as I sprinted full throttle and leapt over the top of the waist-high fire fence. I felt the intense warmth of the fire, but only for a moment. My feet landed with a thud and I felt the shock in my knees. I didn't give myself time to recover. There was a green hosepipe and a brass tap just ahead. And there was a hissing salamander just behind me.

I bounded to the tap in seconds, stabbed my swords into the dirt, aimed the hosepipe's pistol grip at the charging salamander, currently cultivating a flaming booger, and switched on the tap.

Steam and both the pained hisses of the creature and the hisses of water on fire filled the air. I let the water blast it at full throttle and, when I could no longer see its orangey glow through the stream, I drew my swords from the dirt and charged it.

The creature was an extinguished black, breathing hoarsely. I could see ivory white teeth in its maw. It was still salivating lava onto the lawn. Its chest heaved painfully as it lay prostrate, its limbs twisted unnaturally.

"Some monster, Kat."

I wasn't grinning any more.

Treth was right. Some monster...

I still smelled burning. There were open flames in the house. I doubted it could be repaired. A family's life had been ruined.

"Pity the monster, Treth," I said, as I hovered my blades over the creature's head. Its eye, yellow and white, looked up at me. It held no hint of recognition. It was in too much pain for that. "But it is a monster all the same."

I brought my swords down in one, harsh, thrust.

***

A crowd of onlookers was surprised to see me as I left the crackling house, pulling the dead salamander with a chain and hook. The only person who wasn't surprised was a sleazy looking gentleman with dark skin, slicked back hair and a blue business suit.

Conrad Khoi. My monster hunting agent. He found me the jobs, made sure I got paid, and made my life a lot easier in a bloody profession. I had learnt to stop caring about his less than becoming façade a while ago. Conrad may be in it for the money (like me, to an extent) but he was a good person at heart. I felt I could trust him.

Conrad grinned widely with a row of pearly whites and brought his hands together to clap. Some of the bystanders, a bunch of firemen, cops, neighbours and the distraught family, looked askance at him. A few people instinctively joined the applause but stopped when nobody else joined. Conrad stopped clapping and put his hands in his pockets. With one final heave, I pulled the salamander in front of us.

"Gratz, Kat!" he said. "First drake kill?"

I nodded. Drakes were a subset of fire breathing reptiles. They ranged from salamanders, like this one, to titanic dragons.

Conrad squatted down by the beast and gazed intently at the salamander. I'm not really sure why. Was he making sure it was dead? I sure hope it was dead. I stabbed it in the head with two sharp blades. Well, I'd done the same with the vampire barman at the Quantum. Even cut his head off. He appeared on TV only a few days afterwards. Some monsters are really hard to kill.

"You didn't damage the hide," Conrad said. I heard a hint of respect in his voice.

"Clean kill – after I gave it a wash."

Conrad stood. "I had a freelancer back in the day. First guy I hired. A sorcerer with an affinity for axes. He killed a salamander straight out of a rift as well."

I shifted my weight. My muscles ached from the exertion. At least I didn't have any severe burns.

"This guy, we called him the Spell-Axe, took the salamander's hide and had it turned into a coat."

"A benefit of hunting drakes. Imagine if I was to skin and wear the skin of my usual prey."

Conrad laughed. "Wouldn't provide much in the way of protection."

He reached out and touched me. I didn't flinch. He was feeling a piece of my leather jacket, which I now noticed had been burnt. Only the internal padding had stopped the burning completely, but it was now crumbling. Wouldn't take a wight's blade or even a zombie's claw in its current state. Would need to replace it – again!

"Howabout I take this fella." He indicated the salamander as one might a dog. "And get a coat made for you?"

I raised my eyebrow. "Cost?"

We usually sold the corpses of monsters for an extra paycheque. Drake corpses were especially valuable. Scientists were still trying to figure out what made them tick, alchemists needed them for potions and magicorps liked to sell the parts to both the former.

"Still gonna sell the insides. Don't worry about the rest of the cost. I'll cover it."

That was a shock. Conrad, the money grubbing fixer who didn't do a thing without money involved, getting a gift made for me?

"Not like you, Conrad. Getting sentimental?" I snickered.

"Let's say I am," he said, seriously. "I'm sentimental about my investments. And you are an investment that has paid well. Might as well double-down."

"Well, thanks…" I said in a mock offended tone. I wasn't insulted. Was actually flattered. If I was a good investment, it meant I was doing a good job. I was proud of my work.

The onlookers had begun to disperse, except for a few firemen and the family. An ash-covered woman was weeping, her son trying to comfort her. He was too young to really understand how bad things were and a child always hated to see their parents cry.

I didn't speak to them. I always hated speaking to the victims. Had to do it a lot and it never became any easier, or useful. I didn't expect thanks from them either. The deed had been done. I couldn't stop the salamander from destroying their home. Couldn't stop the zombies from eating that man's family. Couldn't stop the mysterious Necrolord who now dominated the slums of my city.

"Conrad…" I began.

"This about the Necrolord?"

He reading my mind? He was getting as bad as Treth. Was I really that open?

I nodded, reluctantly.

Conrad sighed. "The Necrolord isn't our concern, Kat. He is keeping his head down."

During my middle-year break between semesters, a cartel of vampires tried to summon one of their dark gods onto Earth. My friend, Trudie, had been one of the sacrifices, intended to coax the Ancient Vampire onto my world. Well, she would have been if I hadn't gotten to her first. But I didn't have my detective skills to thank for finding her. I'm a pretty shoddy detective. Rather, I had made a deal with the devil. A necromancer. The same necromancer who had attacked me months before when I was doing a job by the North Road, had given me the information I needed in exchange for leaving them alone. I was desperate. My best friend was missing. Can you blame me?

Well, doesn't matter. I blame myself. I let a lot of people die, and now a dark shadow loomed over the slums of Hope City. And it was growing ever larger.

"Undead attacks have grown rarer and rarer, Kat. Last week alone, the only undead sightings were rift-borne."

He frowned as he saw that I was still brooding.

"The Necrolord is probably dead..."

"No. Not them. They're much too big for that."

"How do you know?"

I shrugged. "A gut feeling. I trust my gut."

Conrad sighed, heavier than any sigh he'd given before.

"Things are calm at the moment, Kat. Enjoy it. You must get tired of smelling like rotting flesh and blood all day."

Things were calm at the moment. Calm for Hope City, that is. But I couldn't help but feel this was the calm before the storm, and believe me, a storm was coming.

Chapter 2. Class

Classes this semester were much more pleasant than the last. They started later, for one. Usually, I'd get a few minutes of sleep after hunting all night and then be woken up for my morning lecture. Sometimes by my alarm, sometimes by Treth, and sometimes by Duer, the pixie who lives in my apartment. But this new timetable was much more forgiving. So, forgiving, in fact, that I had time to go home and wash the stench of fire off me before heading up to campus.

Secondly, this semester I was studying a module in Vampire Lore. I had previously not been looking forward to it, but after the disappearance of my old lecturer, the university had hired Miriam LeBlanc, an old employer of mine and a world-class expert on vampirism. Her classes were also my reason for getting up in the morning.

Unfortunately, I didn't have her today. Rather, I was sitting through the drudgery of history. Don't get me wrong. I love history, but this lecturer was a bore. He made something as interesting and as complex as the Sintari invasion of Auckland into a grind. I should just bunk his classes and read a book about it. Would be much more valuable. But, I always met Trudie for lunch in one of the campus's cafeterias. It was a tradition that I enjoyed and could sit through a dull class once a day to keep up.

There was one thing I didn't like about campus this semester, however. Andy. My one-time crush, and now someone I didn't want to see - ever. Being on campus, and him being a class mate of both Trudie and Pranish didn't help my cause. Trudie still liked him, after what he'd done (or more accurately, not done), but she didn't remember a thing about what had happened. Was unconscious the entire time. All she knew was that she had been kidnapped and that her club buddy, Stephanie, was dead, and there was no body. Pranish, on the other hand, hated the guy. He never said it outright, but I saw it in his eyes. Pranish never showed his anger the way I did. I hit and stab things when I'm angry. Pranish stands up and walks away. He tenses his fist. He avoids eye contact.

I used to think it was because my friend was weak, but I knew better now. Pranish had helped me save Trudie. He'd flung spells that's very use hurt his mind and body. And he now lived with the trauma of that day and night. I saw it in his blank stares when he thought no one was looking. I saw it in the way he forgot to smooth his collar sometimes. How Trudie now had to remind him to tuck in his shirt, the way he used to.

Pranish had been changed. Andy had not. And for Andy's idleness, we despised him.

Some would accuse me of holding a spark for Andy, despite his refusal to help us. Some would cite sexual tension and other pseudo-psychological nonsense. They'd be wrong. Andy had betrayed me. I don't deal with traitors.

But, I do compromise. And Andy was friends with Trudie. For that, he was allowed to sit at our table. Pranish left when he couldn't handle it any more.

I entered one of the smaller cafeterias on upper campus after class to the sight of Trudie and Andy. Pranish stopped beside me. He was in the same class as Trudie and Andy, so must've been walking very slowly, waiting for me to arrive.

"Hey," I said, cheerfully.

"Hey," he said back, not so cheerfully. He was glaring at Andy.

He leant in. Trudie and Andy hadn't seen us at the door yet.

"Why does she still hang out with him?" Pranish hissed.

"Because she wasn't awake to be angry. Don't blame her. She's innocent."

Pranish didn't respond. Didn't argue. How could he? We wanted Trudie to be innocent. Well, as innocent as a punky, fun-loving twenty-year-old goth girl could be. Sure, she partied hard, drank as much as she could (very little, she's a lightweight) and may or may not be doing some sort of semi-prohibited substances, but at least she hadn't seen what we'd seen. For that, we were thankful.

"Well, let's go in," I said. Pranish grunted.

Trudie beamed as she saw us, white teeth contrasting with black lipstick. Andy smiled in greeting as well. I sincerely smiled at Trudie and gave a half-arsed smile to Andy. Pranish only smiled at Trudie and avoided looking at Andy.

Pranish and I sat down, flanking Trudie, with Andy on the other side. Trudie frowned, as it became obvious that we were keeping our distance. But she didn't mention it. Much too classy for that. Andy did grimace, slightly, but then returned his face to his normal passive smile. I used to find it charming. Now it was just irritating. Insincere. He looked plastic.

Trudie sniffed and then scowled.

"You been starting fires in your living room?"

"Something like that."

Thought a shower, shampoo and deodorant would have gotten the stink out!

"What type of monster makes one smell like fire?" Andy asked, grinning mischievously, the way he used to. When would he get a clue? He wasn't welcome here anymore.

"The now dead kind," Pranish said, considering his sandwich.

"You know about it?" Trudie asked Pranish.

Pranish shrugged. "It's Kat. Obviously, she was hunting monsters."

Trudie rolled her eyes. She still didn't like my work, was worried about me, but had gotten less naggy about it. A shame. I kinda missed the attention.

"So, Pranish," Andy said, still maintaining his cordial tone. "How's your prac going?"

"Fine."

Silence.

"Pranish is working out a way to program enchantments into code," Trudie said, trying to enthuse the group and eliminate boundaries. Ah, such a wonderful and innocent girl. Too bad it wouldn't work to shift Pranish and my sentiments.

"Very cool," Andy said. "Doing Shard Industries proud."

Andy was referring to Pranish's family business, a highly successful magicorp – a corporation that specialised in magic.

"Haven't told them about it," Pranish muttered through some mouthfuls.

Andy, evidently bored with Pranish, turned to me. "So, any good hunts?"

I tensed my hands underneath the table. Was it any of his business? No! But Trudie was looking at me. Her look was telling me to play nice. I bit down on my temper and replied.

"Had a sword fight with a wight the other day. He was pretty good, too. Was dressed all up in Renaissance fencing garb. Had a rapier and all."

Trudie looked away. She didn't like me talking shop.

"What happened?" Andy pressed.

I shrugged. "I was better. Broke his sword in half and then spit his head on the remains."

Trudie's lip quivered and I stopped. Andy's face remained unchanged. Did he not notice that this topic hurt Trudie, or did he not care?

Pranish stood before I could.

"Got work to do," he muttered, and left.

Trudie sighed and stood up to follow him, leaving me alone with Andy.

Before he could speak, I blurted out some vague excuse that I cannot recall and then departed.

My phone rang as I left. Conrad.

"Job?" I asked. No pleasantries.

"No rush," he replied. "Finish your classes and whatever and meet me at the Titan Citadel. This is a big one."

He hung up.

It was always a big one, but this time, it must be a really big one. Titanic, even.

Chapter 3. Citadel

The Titan Citadel was a huge spire built on top of Table Mountain. It cast a long shadow over Hope City and, if the pre-Cataclysm old timers were to be believed, severely hurt the old skyline of what used to be Cape Town.

It was a necessary evil, however. Under Table Mountain, awakened by the Vortex that brought magic into our world, was the titan Adamastor, a primordial titan once believed to only be the creation of a Portuguese poet. But the earthquakes that had erupted at his almost awakening three decades ago were anything but poetic. Only the swift creation of the Titan Citadel and the establishment of the Titan Order had saved Hope City, and possibly the world. They kept the titan asleep, for now.

A cult had since formed around the Titan Under the Mountain, setting up shrines around the mountain and praying for it to continue its mercy and its slumber. They were a bunch of loonies, but I hadn't been alive to witness the Titan's fury. They had. So, I gave them a bit of the benefit of the doubt. Even if their chants and preaching kept me awake every Saturday morning.

Scholars didn't know if the Titan had appeared after the Vortex or was merely awakened by it, but that didn't matter. All that mattered to the administration of Hope City and the Titan Magi was keeping the beast asleep, so that the city and the world could survive a bit longer without being stomped on by a storm-bringing colossus.

I had grown up my entire life with the Titan Under the Mountain. For me, it was as normal as the Capetonians of old waking up and seeing Table Mountain without a dark tower on it. I had always been sceptical of the Titan, the cult and even the cause to keep it asleep but had always had larger concerns. The Council did a lot worse than fund the Titan Magi and there were much more prominent threats to Hope City than state-sponsored sorcerers.

I met Conrad in a parking lot half-way up Table Mountain, by the cable station meant to take us to the Citadel. The taxi was able to drive up to this point on a mountainside road, dominated by a fortress bustling with red-robed Titan cultists and navy-blue clad cops and security forces. The Citadel was a national key point and was strictly guarded. Only confirmed cultists were given the right to climb to the top of the mountain for their pilgrimage. Otherwise, it was just the Titan Magi allowed to ascend to the top. Well, until now.

"Excited?" Conrad asked, leaning up against his banged-up Golf – his car and, seemingly, his home.

I shrugged. "Never thought I'd go up to the Citadel, so never got excited about the possibility. Do you know anything about the case?"

"Not much. The Titan Magi don't like tech. Got one of their liaisons to call me. Something about disappearances."

I sighed, heavily. "Not another one. That mimic case was bad enough."

"Hey, if it is a mimic again, at least then you know how to deal with it."

"If it doesn't eat me when I try to toast bread in it."

We left Conrad's car and proceeded to a two-storey concrete structure reinforced with polished steel plating. A bullet-proof glass double-door at the base of the structured was flanked by two guards. The one was holding onto a sub-machine gun, while the other had his hands in his pockets. His confident smirk and calm manner belied a man who had never had to struggle or work for power. A sorcerer. Both men wore a simple white shield logo on their jackets. As was to be expected from the logo, the pair were from an agency called Whiteshield. While Puretide and Drakenbane were agencies who specialised in monster hunting, Whiteshield specialised against more human targets. The Council used them to guard key points, backup the cops against rioters and act as bodyguards of important figures.

While the cops were incompetent and corrupt, unable and unwilling to lift a finger to help the people of Hope City, Whiteshield were scarily efficient. Like all private companies, they only got paid when they did their job properly – so they ensured they always did their job properly.

"Khoi. Conrad," Conrad said when we arrived at the door. The SMG-wielding guard glared at us while the sorcerer pulled out a tablet computer and slowly scrolled through some apps. He wasn't in any rush. Was taking his sweet time. It was all an act, of course. He was showing us that he was above us. That he was allowed to waste our time. It wasn't the behaviour of someone near the site of a monster attack.

Finally, the guard stopped and pointed at me.

"Kat Drummond," I said, not hiding my disdain.

He inclined his head and indicated for us to pass. The SMG guard opened the door and we entered.

The entry-hall of the building was big, rising to the second storey. Its floor was mottled tiles and its walls were a smooth black. A sculpture dominated the centre. It was cast-iron, double my size and depicted a muscular and veiny hand grasping towards the ceiling. A plaque underneath read:

"He sleeps. For now."

Very ominous.

Conrad stared at the plaque for just a little too long. I examined his face and he was deep in thought.

How old was he? Was he around to witness the Titan's initial fury? Underneath the cosmetics, how old was my agent?

"Mr Khoi?" a woman said, sending echoes across the hard floor as she walked with her high heel shoes. Our heads swivelled towards her. She wore a red trouser suit and sunglasses, even though we were indoors, and it was cloudy. Her dark blonde hair was tied up in a short ponytail. On her lapel, she wore an iron pin in the shape of the hand sculpture dominating the hall.

Conrad shook the woman's hand.

"You must be our liaison."

She bowed her head and then offered her hand. "And this must be Miss Drummond. I am Charlotte McAbee. Titan Citadel Liaison."

"A pleasure," I said. I felt a tinge of amusement from Treth.

"Sucking up?" Treth asked, a hint of a chuckle in his voice.

"I act as one of the connections for the Magi to the outside world. Normally, it would be against protocol to bring a non-Citadel or non-Cult member to the peak, but this is an unusual situation."

"Tell us what we need to know, Charlotte," Conrad said her first name as if he was familiar with her, but it was evident that they'd only just met. Was he flirting with her? A small twist of his lip suggested that he was. A time and a place, Conrad!

Charlotte shook her head. "I will leave that to Cornelius. He is the HR manager at the Citadel. He will explain everything you need to know about the…case."

She said the last word very reluctantly.

"Before then, please follow me. I will explain some crucial information on the way."

She eyed my swords.

"Usually, one would not be allowed to bring weapons near the Magi, but you are a special exception, Ms Drummond. Let us hope that you are a smart exception."

"I will behave, Ms McAbee."

She stared at my impassive face for a long while and then nodded. She turned and walked towards the opposite side of the hall, through a glass sliding door that opened automatically at her approach. Conrad and I followed.

"This lady has special permission to bring her weapons to the peak," Charlotte said to a Whiteshield guard.

"This is against proto..."

"Protocol changes, sergeant," she snapped.

The sergeant nodded. Wasn't willing to argue. Charlotte was his employer. She made the rules – and changed them at a whim, it seems.

Just past the sergeant and a metal detector checkpoint was a blue metal box with windows. The cable car. Before the Cataclysm, the cable car was a big tourist attraction for foreign and local visitors alike. Anyone wanting to get to the top of Table Mountain, without too much of a sweat, needed to take it. Today, it was the only way to get up to the mountain without being shot at by Whiteshield. Fences and guard posts jealously guarded all the hiking and climbing points up the mountain. It was a shame. I had enjoyed hiking when I didn't get my exercise in more dangerous ways and had always wanted to hike this prohibited mountain that dominated my city.

The hydraulic doors of the cable car hissed as they opened. Charlotte entered, and we followed. The inside of the box was spacious, with metal hand-rails by the windows to hold on. Conrad grabbed onto a railing, but Charlotte did not. I followed her example, but as the box heaved, I was almost flung off my feet. Charlotte was busy looking at her phone. How was she balancing so perfectly on this earthquake simulator while wearing high-heels? Madness! I grabbed onto the railing and looked out the window as the car rose from the station like it was ascending to heaven.

I'd never been this high up before, and we had only just begun the ascent. I could already see Old Town in all its historical splendour and magical prosperity. Its shining blue and steel skyscrapers, pre and post Cataclysm, rose up into the sky, attracting birds and a small group of drakes. Drakenbane was probably en route to exterminate the relatively harmless flying reptiles. Couldn't have them scaring executives in their high rises. Past Old Town was the ocean and, a bit more inland, the Southern Suburbs, where I lived. It was a mish-mash of newer magicorp towers similar to those in Old Town, and a sea of suburban housing and parks. Despite new developments to tap into weylines, the parks of Hope City survived. These places of nature and joy were necessary for healthy weylines, after all.

We ascended higher and higher, and details became blurrier, but I could see further. The North Road, where I had met the necromancer who tormented me for the first time, and the slums in the distance, covered in a thick layer of magical and non-magical smog. Somewhere in that sea of decay was my foe. The necromancer, now called the Necrolord. They had used me, toyed with me, and they were still out there.

I looked away from the sickening and distant sight of the slums and looked down at the increasingly steeper slopes of the mountain. They were covered in thriving green foliage and grey boulders. Table Mountain had a strong weyline, and it was easy to see this now. While nature attracted weylines, weylines also encouraged nature. And nature was flourishing here. I wished the windows could open, so I could smell the freshness, but they looked to be bolted shut.

"Never seen that expression on your face before," Conrad said. He had sidled up next to me. Charlotte was on the opposite end of the cable car, speaking quietly on the phone.

"And what expression is that?"

"Wonder, perhaps."

"We don't spend time around each other much. A lot of new things to discover," I said sharply. Conrad didn't seem to care.

"He's right, you know?" Treth added.

"We spend so much time looking at the horror that it is hard to remember the simple things we are fighting to protect," Conrad continued, staring out into the distance, almost wistfully.

I snorted. "We both remember to collect the simple things after completion and then deposit them in the bank."

Conrad let out a small chuckle. "Profit is one of those wonderfully simple things, but it's not just that…"

He looked out onto the city. While he had never seen me show wonder before, I had never seen this expression from him. A forlornness brought about from memory perhaps?

"I'm not from Hope City, but I've been here so long that it is my home. Used to be that I stayed here cause the money was good. But it ain't as good any more. Then, why do I stay?"

He was half-talking to himself, in a hushed whisper. He didn't look away from the city. Before I could say anything, the car heaved to a stop. The hum of its engine ceased and we heard clicks as it locked into place. We were now in a shadow, bringing an unnatural coolness to the car. The hydraulics hissed, and the doors opened. We exited.

It was windy outside. Hope City was always windy, but this was on another level. Without the resistance of buildings and trees, the wind on the peak of Table Mountain was punishing. My hair, despite being tied up in a ponytail, went crazy, sending wisps of dark chestnut into chaos.

The shadow, I saw now, was formed by the Citadel itself. Just past another cable-station, identical to the grey block we had just come from, was a looming black tower, casting a night-like shadow over us. I couldn't tell what material the tower was made from. It didn't look like stone, brick or metal. The closest thing it could be was void-black marble, yet that also wasn't right. I had learnt about the magical origins of the Citadel in history, but textbook descriptions didn't do the structure justice. It didn't look like it was from this world, yet it had been crafted by human mages. Well, it didn't come from this world then. Magic was pretty otherworldly.

There were two more armed guards standing by the car. They weren't Whiteshield, however, but wore the red of the Titan Cult. They eyed Conrad and me with unrestrained suspicion but didn't speak or make a move on us. I kept my arms crossed, so not to scare them by having my hands too close to my swords. They looked jumpy. Didn't want to make them jump at my expense.

Charlotte indicated for us to proceed by entering through the sliding doors of this station. We followed. Inside this building was a carbon copy foyer of the one below, sculpture and all. We didn't waste any time, and passed right through, to a windy stretch of shrubbery, rocks and a dirt path leading up to the gargantuan black tower. Charlotte stopped to take off her shoes. The path must be too rocky for high heels, despite her adept balance. She replaced the high-heels with some hard slippers left by the door. She must do this a lot. Appearances were important in her line of business, and she felt high-heels were needed for the image they presented.

The trip from the station to the entrance of the Citadel was silent. We didn't speak, as we could not, over the buffeting of the wind. We stopped by the door of the Citadel, a somewhat normal looking metal door with a security camera above it. Charlotte pressed a button by the door and looked up towards the camera. With a buzz, the door unlocked, and we entered.

The room before us was a darkly lit space, with rugs and Impressionist landscape paintings spread across the black surfaces, attempting to bring a bit of warmth to the cold area. In the centre of the room was a wooden, crescent desk. At a computer by it, a landline telephone to his ear, was a man in about his thirties, with light stubble, messy brown hair and round-rimmed glasses.

Charlotte went to him and tapped her fingers impatiently on the desk. He held up his finger, nodded and then hung up.

"So, Charlotte. Good afternoon to you too," the man said with a hint of a childlike grin. I decided that I liked this man. He seemed more human than anyone else I'd seen wearing the red of the Titan Cult.

"Cornelius, these are the monster hunters."

He looked past her at Conrad and me, adjusted his glasses and frowned. Frowned at me. Wasn't the first time it had happened. People weren't used to a 19-year-old girl slaying monsters. And, while I had a reputation in the monster hunting community, Hope City was a big place and most people had never heard of me.

The man stood and offered his hand. "I'm Cornelius Black, chamberlain of the Titan Citadel. Please follow me to the briefing room."

Charlotte had already left without a word. What an odd lady.

"Don't mind Charlotte," Cornelius said, cheerily, as we walked. "She's never not working. No time for pleasantries. She is responsible for the survival of everyone in the Citadel, after all. Grocery shopping for two-hundred men and women is not an easy task."

He led us into a small sitting room where I immediately felt something sharp scrape through my shirt and into my arm. I'd felt worse before, but the surprise made me stop.

"You're bleeding!" Cornelius said, shocked. "My apologies. The design of this building does not make sense most of the time. Some of the walls have decorative spikes. No one knows why, and we cannot remove them. The materials of this building are indestructible after all. Just what we get for summoning what doesn't belong into our world…"

He stopped thoughtfully for a second. I examined my arm. There was an inch long cut dripping blood onto my t-shirt. Didn't really hurt, but I was upset about my t-shirt. Clothes were expensive.

Cornelius' gaze locked onto me and the cut on my arm.

"Oh! Sorry. Let me get you something for that cut."

I put up my hand to pre-empt his fussing. "No, it's fine. Really. Nothing compared to the usual."

He came anyway and, despite my apprehension, wiped the blood off my arm with a tissue. I frowned and then shrugged. Conrad had already taken a seat on a plush, blue sofa.

Cornelius halted his nervous first-aid and made way for me to find a place to sit. I sat on an armchair near Conrad, leaving another sofa opposite us for Cornelius.

"I trust that Charlotte didn't give any details?"

Conrad and I nodded.

"Good. Well, I don't know how she would tell you the details. She doesn't know herself."

"So, this is top secret then?" Conrad asked.

"Yes, Mr Khoi," a new voice answered. "Top secret and very, very sensitive."

As I turned to see the new arrival, I caught a flash of intense displeasure on Cornelius' face. Interesting.

Cornelius stood. "This is the meister of the Citadel, Stephen DuPreez."

The man didn't smile. If anything, his scowl seemed deep etched into his face. He had short, white hair, yet didn't look a day over forty. It wasn't that white of age, but more a snow-white that indicated some sense of wisdom or power. I could feel a distant hum of electricity from him. I often felt it around sorcerers of immense power. The meister was powerful. More powerful than any sorcerer I had ever had the displeasure of meeting before.

He didn't offer his hand. Conrad didn't seem to care. He only reclined further back onto the sofa, looking like he owned the place.

"Meister, I was just about to explain the…situation…to the hunters."

43

"Don't you have procurement forms to fill in, Chamberlain?" Stephen said with a hint of finality that overwhelmed the words themselves. He was telling Cornelius to leave.

I saw Cornelius' lip twitch, and then he bowed low and left. Stephen took Cornelius' seat and leaned back, steepling his fingers, while his elbows rested on the arms of the chair.

"Mr Khoi, it has been awhile."

"It has, Steve."

Conrad said the meister's name with a casualness that made the sorcerer flinch. To my knowledge, Conrad didn't know any wizardry and wasn't a sorcerer. He wasn't rich (he lived out of a Golf!) and he wasn't a good fighter. Yet, he was calling this man who could melt him with his mind "Steve". My respect for my boss grew ten-fold instantly.

"Last time we saw each other, you were explaining why I should still pay you and your freelancers for killing that cyclops despite the battle destroying my estate."

Conrad shrugged. "You knew my team's reputation. You chose to hire them in spite of that."

Stephen's scowl deepened. "Ten silver plates were unaccounted for after the battle."

Conrad's mouth almost twitched up into a smile.

"Collateral damage," he said, simply.

There was a tense silence, and then Stephen's eyes shifted to me.

"I asked the liaison to contact you because, despite your propensity for theft and vandalism, you get the job done. But if I had known that you were going to bring a high school girl, I would have called an agency."

High school girl! I'm taller than most of my friends. The comment didn't seem to disturb Conrad, however, who grinned subtly, yet enough to ruffle Stephen's feathers.

"Kat is already one of my top tier hunters, Steve. She has killed countless undead and vampires, she slew a salamander this morning and put down a necromancer approaching lichdom."

Lichdom? That was pushing it a bit. Jeremiah was powerful, but not that powerful. Still, I didn't tell Stephen that.

"Besides," Conrad's grin became more obvious now. "If you could contact an agency, you would have already. This is too sensitive for that. Too sensitive to let anyone from Whiteshield, Drakenbane or Puretide know about.

Perhaps, because the Council has more ears than you'd like — and this is not something you want the Council to know about…"

The pair locked eyes. Stephen gave in first and looked away. He leaned back in his chair and addressed both of us.

"For the past few weeks, eight Titan mages have disappeared under violent circumstances. There is no sign of struggle, despite evidence of extreme violence. Our surveillance shows nothing useful and our magic detectors have recorded no use of hostile magic. This leads me to believe that the culprit is a monster."

He snapped his fingers and a hazy screen appeared before us, melding into the air. It was surveillance footage, time-stamp and all. It was filmed around 4am. It showed a small but comfortable looking room, with a man sleeping in its single bed. The footage sped up, evident by the time-stamp and the hasty tossing and turning of the sleeper. Then it slowed down. One second, the man was there, the next, he was gone, leaving a blood splattered room.

Stephen snapped his fingers again and the shimmering, incorporeal screen disappeared.

"As you said, Mr Khoi, this is a sensitive matter. We cannot let the Titan Cult know about this, much less the Council. If they knew that Titan Mages were disappearing, or being murdered, there would be general panic. Possible defunding. And that is the least of our worries. The Cult is useful for our purposes, but if they believe that we cannot keep the Titan under control, there will be rebellion. Do I need to spell out what that means?"

No. He did not. Rebellion would mean an end to the tenuous Titan Citadel. And, if they were to be believed,the subsequent awakening of the Titan Under the Mountain.

"Kat will find your monster, Steve," Conrad said, without consulting me. "Then, she'll put it down."

I was happy about the confidence he was putting in me, but I wasn't so sure myself.

Chapter 4. Range

"I don't like it, Kat," Treth said, as we walked up a dirt path towards the sounds of gunfire.

"You don't like a lot of things these days," I responded. Treth was upset about the Citadel case. He thought our time would be better spent slaying the endless undead. I partly agreed with him. I didn't like these detective-work cases. They took too long. They occupied too much of my mind that should be dedicated to studying. But, more than that, they made me feel powerless. My skill-set was stabbing, not protracted investigation. But, it couldn't be helped. I needed to be the detective. While I felt unable to solve a case, how did the non-hunters feel? I may not feel suited to this, but I was much better suited to it than they who didn't know the difference between a ghoul and a wraith.

"We should be investigating the necromancer," Treth continued. I frowned. I agreed, but it couldn't be helped. There were no leads on the necromancer and no one paying me to look for them. I wanted to stop them, but still needed to pay the rent and tuition.

"Consider this practice, Treth. If we can find an invisible mage murderer, we can find the necromancer."

And then what?

Put them down, like I did Jeremiah?

Could I kill a human again?

Would I have a choice?

The sight of Brett shook me out of my reverie as I passed an open wooden gate and saw the muscle-bound back of my obnoxious friend. He was wearing a tight black AC/DC t-shirt. On his one arm was a tattoo of a skull impaled on a knife. On the other were just the numbers 56-3. His hair was short, making him look the part of a military veteran. I didn't know much about my friend's past, but I wouldn't be surprised if he had a military background. When we came across the vampire cartel's ritual to summon one of their dark gods onto Earth, he had not only survived an attack from a pack of monstrous vampires that seemed impervious to harm, but also helped distract the vampires with the adept use of frag grenades.

Brett was also a monster hunter but worked for the Drakenbane agency. For a long time, he irritated me, but after helping me save my friend, Trudie, from vampires, he was very high up in my books. High enough that I had even asked him to teach me how to shoot. During that escapade with the vampire, I had felt out of my depth.

Sure, I can hunt ghouls and stupid vampiric monsters, but these vampires had guns. What would I have done about that if Brett and his partner, Guy, had not come to help me? I'd be dead. And, so would Trudie. And if Miriam and the necromancer who tormented me were to be believed, so would the world.

So, here I am, a swordswoman about to learn how to shoot.

Brett had told me to come to this range because it was typically empty during the week. He was right. The small little firing range was located in a quarry, ensuring no misfires found someone to hit. The targets backed onto the dirt-mounds and there was no way to get there unless you jumped the tables by a small sheltered strip, where the shooters stood, and charged across the firing line. Brett and I were alone in the quarry, so I didn't expect any accidental casualties, unless one of us lost our senses.

Brett stopped firing and took off his ear-protectors. He was checking over his pistol as I approached. The sound of my shoes on the sand made him twitch and he turned. For a second, I saw a look of grim anticipation on his face, but then it broke. He smiled.

"Katty! Glad you could make it."

He always called me Katty. Probably because he knew I didn't like it.

I shrugged. "Of course. Not going to say no to free training and free ammo."

"Of course." He grinned. "No one as smart as you would."

"Starting the flattery already, Brett?"

He put the pistol down on the table. "Only flattery if it ain't true."

"Doubling down?"

He laughed and fished into a backpack hanging on a hook. He took out a holster containing a pistol. Don't ask me what type. I'm not a gun person – yet. Ask me about swords though. I can tell you a lot about those.

"Usually, I'd start a first timer with a lower calibre, but you aren't in this just to shoot paper targets and birds. So, a baptism of fire is a lot better. 9mm are not too big a jump but will still ring your shoulder the first few times. It's also the most common calibre you'll use, so good to get used to."

He handed me the gun and holster. I drew it out and examined it. I had seen it before. A lot of cops and monster hunters used them.

"That's a Glock 17. 9mm. Semi-auto. That means…"

"I've never fired a gun in real life, but I've played enough video games to know what that means."

Brett nodded. "It's a good gun. Not going to put down a zombie instantly unless you get a really good headshot, but you don't need help putting down zombies."

"How will it fare against vamps?"

Brett looked away, back at his gun on the table. His expression and tone darkened. "Nothing does well against vamps. Best you can do is put in silver shot or a silver hollow-point. Solid silver will go right through and won't affect their regeneration. Need the silver to stay in the wound to stop it from growing back."

"So, how'd you kill those garkains?

I heard a series of clicks as Brett inserted a magazine into his pistol and pulled back the slide. It gave a satisfying click as the round chambered.

"My ace," he said, simply. "Well, aces. When you said we were going after vampires, I made sure I brought them."

He held out his hand and I passed him the Glock. He checked over it and continued.

"Silver frag grenades. Normal pineapple 'nades, but chock-full of silver shrapnel."

"Bullets and my blades just glanced off those monsters. Silver needs to interact with their blood to stop the regeneration. It doesn't really make the weapon stronger against vampires, it just stops the regeneration," I said, channelling Miriam LeBlanc.

Brett nodded. "You know quite a bit about vamps. Thought they wouldn't interest you. They don't smell like year-old trash."

"I've got a good teacher," I answered. "So, how did you use the grenades?"

Brett indicated for me to take a space beside him at the range stall. He took a loaded magazine out of a container and inserted it into the Glock.

"I pretended to fall," he said, no hint of his usual humour. He was describing business, in a very business-like fashion. "And as it opened its mouth to feed, I shoved a grenade down its gullet."

"And you still have your arm?" I asked, genuinely impressed. I don't think I could do anything like that. My respect for Brett grew tenfold.

"I pulled out in time."

He said it seriously, but then smirked. I stared at him with an expression that I hoped could melt an ice giant. If he wasn't holding a loaded firearm, I would have shoved him.

He put the Glock on the table and made space for me to enter the stall. I rolled my eyes, and advanced. The stall was big enough for the two of us to stand apart comfortably. Brett leaned up against the plastered brick-wall and looked me up and down. I first thought it was the predatory gaze of an admirer, but then he spoke.

"You sure about this?"

"Why wouldn't I be?"

"You used to be squeamish about the idea of killing anything other than undead."

"Things change."

He nodded. "People change, yeah. But you need to understand that guns don't work well on the dead. They're just good at making things dead. You can kill a lot of things with them. Could even kill a zombie with enough lead, but that's not why you're here…"

"Let's learn to shoot, Brett," I said with a hint of finality that he ignored. He put his hand on the Glock as I reached for it.

"If you were just wanting to learn to shoot for sport, I'd smile as we unloaded a few mags into those cut-outs. But I see it in your eyes."

He paused. "And your posture."

I looked up at him. He had real concern in his face. Didn't think I'd ever see it from him.

"Kat, I need to know that this is what you want."

I didn't lift my hand off the Glock. I looked at the range, at the cut-outs that were vaguely human-shaped.

I didn't need a gun to kill the undead, and guns weren't the best thing against vampires. Even then, I'd shown just how well I could kill vampires without a gun already. Brett knew this. He knew that I knew it.

"You don't need it, Kat," Treth said, voice soft and, just a bit, pleading.

I didn't need it. I could walk away. I also didn't need my swords. Didn't need to be a monster hunter. Didn't need to risk my life slaying beasts. I could live a normal life. That'd make Trudie happy.

I looked at the Glock. It wasn't a weapon made to kill the beasts of the Cataclysm. It was designed to kill humans. The humans I'm paid to protect. But not all of them.

Some humans are monsters.

I looked Brett in the eyes and nodded, once. He nodded back and let go.

"Slide that back until it clicks…you cock a gun like a girl."

I glared at him and he grinned, boyishly.

"Hold the gun with both hands, keep your finger off the trigger until you intend to shoot. To aim at your target, line up the front and back sights. Good…"

"Anything else, teach?"

"Squeeze the trigger, don't pull."

I nodded.

"And Kat…"

I looked away from the sights towards him.

"Don't regret this."

***

My shoulder was still aching and my hearing still had the echoes of the bangs, despite my ear-protectors. Brett said you got used to it. I'm sure I would. It wasn't nearly as sore as driving my sword full force into a fleshy looking monster that ended up being as hard as metal. Firing a gun was the type of initial shock you got used to with practice. I spent most of the time firing the gun at the target, getting a feel for the recoil. Brett gave me some pointers, but it was pretty straightforward. Line up the sights and then squeeze the trigger. After some shooting two-handed, he suggested that I practice one-handed, and that I fire as fast as possible. It wasn't something he usually advised but, because my fighting style involved a sword and speed, I should rather be using the pistol in my off-hand, as a support weapon. I fired a bit using one hand, and this was much harder. A lot of my shots went wide, and my shoulder felt like it'd been punched by an orc.

"You'll get better. Any person with an eye-ball can fire a gun at a stationary target while taking ten seconds to aim between shots. But that's not how fighting works," he said, taking a sandwich out of a tin lunchbox and offering one to me. I accepted.

I took a seat next to him, on a dirty bench by the cargo container, and took a bite of the sandwich. It was peanut butter and honey.

"A glorified crossbow," Treth hissed. What was with the disparagement? This was for the cause, even if it was to kill the humans controlling the undead more than the undead themselves.

Brett was still biting into his own sandwich after I finished mine. I always ate too quickly. Treth said it gave me indigestion. I told him he wasn't my mom. Trudie already held that position.

His 56-3 tattoo faced me, illustrated on his tree-trunk arms. It didn't look artsy. Not a fashion statement or some outlet of his creativity. Didn't look like a date either…

"So, Bretty," I said in as playful a tone I could muster. He raised his eyebrow at me, his mouth full of sandwich. I tempered my grin. "What's the tattoo about?"

He stopped chewing and his expression changed. He looked distant. Reluctant. Finally, he swallowed. But, he didn't reply.

I raised my hands diplomatically. "Hey, sorry. No need to talk about it if it is private."

He shook his head. "Nah, nah. It's fine. Just…haven't…yeah, shit."

His words were garbled. Nervous. I'd never seen Brett act like this before. He was normally so cocksure.

"Eh, Katty, won't hurt to tell you. We're alike enough that you'd understand, I think."

I nodded, even though I didn't understand.

Silence.

He sighed, heavily.

"Tattoo means unit 56 of section 3. That was my designation. Very simple. No rank. Simple hierarchy. Soldiers at the bottom and then the Manager, at the top."

"Military?"

He frowned, and the frown went up to his forehead, creasing it. I didn't know how old Brett was, but the wrinkle in his forehead now and the strain in his eyes made him look very old. Very worn out.

"No," he finally said. "Or, not exactly...I was in the Extermination Corps."

To my credit, I didn't gasp. Everybody knew about the Extermination Corps. They were a death squad formed in secret by the oligarchs of the Goldfield Magocracy. Their prime directive was to eliminate non-human sentients. That meant more than just vampires, but also elves, fae, orcs, centaurs, otherworldly humans, even...the list goes on. When non-humans began gaining more sympathy among world governments, the Extermination Corps was discovered and shut down.

"Killed a lot of vampires," Brett continued. "That was the reason I joined, after all. But also killed a lot of elves.

Can't say if they deserved to die or not. Wasn't thinking about that when I did it."

He looked at his feet.

"Very different types of missions than what we do now, Kat. When they did fight back, they shot at me. That's why Guy and I were able to keep our heads cool against those vamp gangsters. We've been shot at a lot. Perhaps, hunting monsters is better. Teeth aren't as fast or as dangerous as a gun. But, I can't help but admit there's something about being shot at that makes a man come alive."

"Was Guy in the Corps?" I asked, ignoring the last disturbing comment. Well, disturbing was unfair. I had to admit that there was something thrilling about coming close to death. Brett was right. We were the same, at least in some ways.

"Guy? Nah. He got his experience leading the Transkei commandos against the Zulus. They sent a vampire clan after his unit and then his village and that's why he's here in Hope City. Nothing left for him in Zulu turf now."

Brett took another sandwich out, offered it to me and then took out his own. We both ate in silence.

So, Brett had killed more than just traditional monsters. He'd killed elves. The people my aunt admired, despite their annexation of half of New Zealand. He'd also killed innocents, by his own implication. But, why? For the sake of my own view of him, I hoped he had a good reason.

"You said you joined the Corps because of vampires?" I asked, another sandwich gone.

"Vampires killed my family," he said. Simply. Matter of factly. As if he had been telling himself that every hour of every day. It was the type of phrase said in the way that revealed that it had become his mantra. His justification for everything.

I realised that Brett and I were, indeed, very much alike. I could not judge him harshly at all for his being in a death squad. If given the opportunity, I may have joined too. For a long time, and maybe even now, I would have done anything to eliminate the undead from this world.

The sun started to fade and Brett offered to take me home. I had a small job nearby, though, so politely declined. He understood and was not offended. He took all the guns with him, of course. I didn't have a license. Was not allowed to have a gun in my possession.

"I don't like this," Treth said again, when we were alone, on the way to the rift-wrought zombie extermination job.

"It's just a zombie."

"Not that. I don't like spending time with that man."

I bit my lip and, instead of scolding the spirit in my head, I just said. "Brett helped us save Trudie."

"He serves vengeance and profit. He helped us so to sate his hatred for vampire-kind."

"That'd be good enough for me," I said, honestly. "But I don't think it was just that. Brett is a good person."

"You didn't always think that."

I shrugged. "People change. In this case, I changed. I grew enough to see past his teasing. He's honourable."

"Honourable, if you pay him enough."

"I've never paid him anything."

"Not yet."

The zombie staggered outside of an alley and I beheaded it with a single swing. It was too far gone for me to know its gender, as its head rolled onto the pavement.

"What are you implying, Treth of Concord?" I evoked his full title like a parent would use the middle name of a misbehaving child.

"He is a man," Treth said. "Men want things."

"You are also a man."

Treth hesitated, then snapped back. "A man without a body. All I want now is the quest."

I sighed, irritated. "So, what if Brett is interested in me? You didn't mind when it was Andy."

A pause. The spirit was wracking his brain for a response. Before he could think of one, I spoke again.

"It isn't Brett, is it? You've been in a bad mood for a while. What's up?"

"Bad mood? Nonsense!" he said, but there was nervousness in his voice. I put my hands on my hips, sword still in my hand, dripping black blood, and glared at nothing in particular. He felt the glare all the same.

"We're effectively one and the same, Treth," I said. "I accepted that a long time ago. No secrets. Or, at least, very few secrets."

"We are both closed books to each other, Kat, and you know it," he snapped, but I felt a sadness in his voice. I sat down on a bench, the zombie corpse unmoving next to us.

"As you've said before, Treth, we're in this together. What's up?"

In the long pause that followed, I could hear birds chirping and the distant crash of waves. I closed my eyes and breathed in the salty sea air. I ignored the stench of undeath next to me.

"Today marks two years that we've known each other."

I froze. I didn't know. Hadn't been keeping track. I burst out laughing. Couldn't help it. It felt so absurd.

"Why are you laughing?" Treth asked, more confused than offended.

"Is that why you are upset? That I forgot our anniversary? Rifts, Treth. We aren't married. I lost count. Been a bit busy."

"It's not that," Treth said, sheepishly. I felt a tinge of sadness emanate from him. I stopped laughing. Shit. I hoped I hadn't offended him. Didn't know he could be sensitive.

"I haven't had a body for that long, Kat," Treth finally said. "Haven't been my own person for that long."

I was about to argue with him as a substitute for actual sympathy but stopped. Treth had always seemed so content with his lot. So certain and accepting that this was his fate and he needed to make the most of it. But was that just a façade? Or had he finally had enough of not being his own man?

"Treth…" I started.

"No, Kat. It's fine. Nothing you or I can do about it. I died. This is just punishment for that failure."

"I hope being in my head isn't that much of a punishment," I tried to joke.

Treth didn't notice that it was a joke. "It isn't a punishment, Kat. For all the people I could have been tethered to, there could be no one better than you."

He sighed.

"I'm sorry for my behaviour," he murmured. "I'll…think things through."

We didn't speak after that while I collected the bounty on the zombie. Throughout, I hoped Treth didn't notice the redness and warmth of my cheeks.

Chapter 5. Patrols

The Titan Citadel was paying me to walk around. Usually, I only got paid when I threw the monster's head at the King's feet and then bowed and scraped for a reward, but there were some benefits to detective-work. Because of its long, drawn-out nature, I was being paid for my time, in addition to the final reward when I solved the case. While this was definitely still not my cup of tea, I certainly did not mind the wage.

My work brought me back to the top of Table Mountain, where I was patrolling around the windswept expanse surrounding the black Citadel. I must say, it was quite pleasant. The day was hot, but the unrestrained wind did wonders to keep me cool and refreshed. The plant-life, called fynbos, was also beautiful this high up. The flora, native to the Cape, were flourishing on top of the mountain, with only the cable station, Citadel and a few footpaths to restrict their growth. It made for a field of green and brightly coloured shrubbery, emitting a faint and pleasant peppery smell. It was a major improvement over the smell of trash, gas and decay down at the mountain's base. This was the true smell of the Cape. The smell of its nature.

"What are we even looking for?" Treth asked. Despite his promises, he had still been cranky on occasion. I chose to ignore his tone. He'd get over whatever it was that was eating him up. Eventually, at least.

"Tracks, disturbances, what doesn't belong..." I said. "The usual. Find the chaos among order. The broken twig in a field of unbroken twigs. Find the outlier and we've found the next step in the investigation."

"Sounds much more complicated than our usual fare."

"Complicated doesn't mean bad."

Treth grunted, but I felt that he was assenting.

I was wading through the brush around the smooth, void black walls of the Citadel. The shrubbery had grown right up against it, leaning on it for support. My investigation brought my gaze up from the foliage below, up the expansive wall next to me. I didn't see any windows. No ventilation holes, either. Cornelius had told me that some sort of magic kept the people inside breathing. That made me uncomfortable. I was only just getting comfortable with magic, but still wasn't near to being comfortable enough to allow it to help me breathe. The lack of air-holes and windows raised a more pertinent question, however.

Something had made Titan mages disappear. But how could anything get into this impenetrable shard of black?

Two possibilities.

It broke through the front door.

Or: it was let in.

I was not sure which was the more terrifying possibility.

I finished rounding the exterior of the Citadel and found no vulnerabilities, signs of tampering or even footprints besides my own. That, at least, narrowed my investigation. Barring something with wings that could pass through walls, the assailant making mages disappear on camera must've come through the only hole in the Citadel – the locked, metal door guarded by a CCTV camera.

I pressed the buzzer by said door and was let through.

"Find anything?" Cornelius asked. He was straightening some paintings. I walked up to him and examined the artwork. It was a Sekoto painting, depicting a pre-Cataclysm South African township. It was colourful, and despite the people's faces being vague representations of their humanity, it held a sense of energy and sincerity.

"Print?" I asked.

Cornelius looked confused and then made an oh with his mouth.

"No, no. This is the original. *Outside the Shop* by Gerard Sekoto."

He finished straightening the, most likely, priceless work of art and examined his handiwork with his hands on his hips.

"So unfortunate that he died so soon after the Vortex. I would have liked to see how he would have depicted what became of his country," Cornelius said.

"Perhaps, it is fortunate for him that he did not. He lived a long life. At least he died when his country was still a country," I replied. I knew a bit about Sekoto. We had done him in school history and he had been mentioned in pre-Cataclysm history.

Cornelius nodded, sadly, and then turned to me.

"So, find anything?"

"I need to see some footage from the front entrance."

Cornelius looked shocked. "Do you think the monster could have gotten through the door?"

"I see no alternative, besides a spirit. And I guess that spirits cannot pass through these void black, otherworldly walls."

Cornelius nodded, confirming my suspicion. The Citadel was impervious to spirits. That left the front door.

"Who could open the front door?" I asked.

"Charlotte, Stephen, and myself," he answered, walking back to his desk and pouring some water from a steaming kettle into two cups.

"Tea?"

"No, thanks," I replied. I had tea with Pranish just before this. He needed some help with his developments in codified enchantments and he rewarded me with rooibos tea and gingernut biscuits.

He stopped pouring and sat down. He didn't continue making his own. I suddenly felt a bit guilty. Just because I didn't want any didn't mean he shouldn't have.

"Don't let me stop you," I said, indicating the kettle.

"No, no. Tea is a social thing. I don't really feel like it. Just a pleasantry."

He smiled, faintly. He was an odd fellow, but likable. Seemed as if he wanted to please people, but not desperately. He wanted to please people for their sakes, not his.

"So," he continued. "Security footage?"

"Yes. I need to see if there is anything out of the ordinary. If spirits can't pass through the walls, and there are no vulnerabilities besides this door, then I can only think that if there is a monster, it came through the front."

Cornelius paled. The thought of a monster coming through the door he stared at all day must be terrifying.

"Could a spirit pass through the front door?" I asked. I was concerned that he was unnerved, but I had a job to do.

"It…it is normal metal alloy. It may have some silver, but I'm not sure," he said, colour returning to his cheeks.

"Anyway, show me the footage, please…"

"None of that, Cornelius. The hunter here is being paid to track down the fiend, not rifle through our sensitive records," Stephen interrupted us, entering the room with a gust of his latent sorcerous energy.

Cornelius looked about to respond, but then looked down at his lap. It was as if he had no will against this sorcerer. Well, I'd need to argue for myself then.

"You are paying me to find a monster. Tracking it may require I look through more than the security footage you have provided me."

"Correct, Ms Drummond. We are paying you. That means that you play by our rules."

I gritted my teeth. "Even if that means the case goes unsolved?"

"Be creative, hunter." He looked at me if I was a child, meant to be scolded.

I sighed. Was he really going to make this more difficult? Regular wage or not, I wanted to be shot of this case eventually.

"Can I ask why?"

"Wizard," Stephen spat, as if it was an insult. "Explain the protocol to the hunter and remind yourself of it while you are at it. I have a meeting with the purifier in my office."

He left as suddenly as he had arrived.

"I don't like him," Treth said. I agreed wholeheartedly.

Cornelius was still looking sheepishly down at his lap, his hands unmoving on the computer keyboard on his desk. He looked beaten. Not physically, but mentally. Was this every day to him? Was this the worst or the best of it? And why?

"Most mages are sorcerers," he whispered. "Me? I'm a wizard. Not much use to them. They channel their energy into keeping the Titan asleep, while I use incantations and rituals to keep the dust away."

"My friend is a wizard," I said. "And he's a better magic-user than any sorcerer I've ever met."

Cornelius didn't smile at that, as I expected he would. Perhaps, I was used to it being easy to cheer people up.

"It isn't about what is better magic. It is about serving the cause. Always the cause. Keep the Titan asleep. Keep him asleep so we don't all die. But, as they constantly remind me, I'm not contributing to the cause. I'm their errand boy. Easily replaceable. Unskilled. Unpowerful..."

If I was in his position, I would have quit a long time ago. But, keep in mind that I work for myself. Not a team player. I don't like bosses. Conrad has only survived so long because he keeps my leash very loose.

"Why stay, then? They obviously don't respect you. Why keep working with them?"

He looked up suddenly, into my eyes and I saw a fire I hadn't seen in his blue eyes before.

"For the cause, Ms Drummond. Damn what they say. I was put on this Earth by God for a reason."

Silence. I, finally, looked down. Cornelius coughed into his hand.

"The protocol that Mr DuPreez reminded me that I have forgotten is that there are many confidential visitors to the Citadel – yourself included. Their anonymity is important to the functioning of this entire venture, so we cannot risk you finding out their identity. Monster or not. I am sorry."

I nodded. "Well, I'll have to do this the old-fashioned way."

He raised an eyebrow.

"Stake-outs, Kat? No matter how far one rises, one must always wait around sometime," a familiar voice said. I turned and saw Cindy Giles, a top-notch purifier and healing mage from Drakenbane and the world-renowned Association of Heiligeslicht. She had helped me save my campus from some rabid necromancer months back, and then testified to get me off for killing said necromancer. She was a good person, as far as I could tell. She was dedicated to her work. So, dedicated that her arms were scarred with the runes she needed to channel her powers.

"Cindy! Didn't expect to see you here," I said, unable to contain a smile. Her presence immediately distracted me from my case. Her funky hair, magically scarred arms and sense of power could do that. I remembered. "I still need to thank you for helping me…with that thing."

Cindy laughed. "It was nothing."

"About that – I heard that you were helping purify an archdemon. How'd it go?"

Cindy's smile waned and was replaced with a furrowed brow and a frown. "Not exactly well."

Cornelius was staring at Cindy with a sense of awe. She wasn't exactly pretty, with her scarred arms, exhausted eyes like mine and lack of make-up, but she was, in a way, awe-inspiring. She was wearing her Heiligeslicht uniform today – a white and gold vestment with the image of a caduceus on the front and the symbol of a lamp hovering over a cross on the back. Heiligeslicht was not a religious organisation, but many of the religious supported them. They were an international association of purifiers, specialising in eliminating curses, demons and dark magic. They were also dedicated to saving orphaned and abused children with spark, to ensure they weren't pressed into magical slavery. Despite my reservations with religion and the religious among their ranks, they were definitely some of the good guys. Cindy being among their ranks made her someone special. Heiligeslicht didn't just accept anyone.

You needed to be totally dedicated to purification magic to even become an acolyte within their ranks.

"My business is done here, Kat," Cindy said. "How about we go for coffee? I know that I need some. We can catch up and share some of our tricks of the trade. I heard you exorcised the spectral horseman of Tokai manor."

I waved away the compliment in her tone.

"He was on the edge of the abyss already. I just reminded him that he was dead. On the topic of coffee — that sounds wonderful."

"Great!" she said. She turned to Cornelius and her tone shifted to business. "Let the Meister know that I will be back in two weeks for another inspection."

Cornelius closed his mouth, nodded, and then muttered some incantation that caused his keyboard to start typing all by itself. Must say, that impressed me. I'd like to see the raw and untamed powers of sorcerers be able to do something that delicate and sophisticated.

"Bye, Cornelius," I said, giving him a smile. I wanted him to have some pleasantry in his life. Being surrounded by bullies was not anyone's idea of fun.

Chapter 6. Coffee

Cindy and I drove to a small coffee shop on the slope of Table Mountain, near Old Town. It was a quaint café with a wrought-iron, cursive sign written in French. Cindy ordered a latte. I ordered a black coffee. We had started speaking in the car and continued after we sat down. The café smelled of lavender.

"...so, after we lost Bernard to spell-shock, the creature broke free of the net and flew away. I hate the ones with wings. They're much harder to contain."

She was explaining the battle with the archdemon at Pinelands. Heiligeslicht, and almost every purifier of some status in the city, had been called out to contain the fiend, but he had overpowered them and escaped. He was now running amok – hopefully, away from the city.

"What could an archdemon do to the city?" I asked, taking a sip of coffee. Cindy didn't look too concerned, so I didn't think it could be too bad.

"It really depends. Demons, and archdemons, all have their own MOs, behaviours, cultures, goals..."

"Know anything about this archdemon?"

She shook her head. "He, she, it...hid themselves in a shroud. They looked vaguely humanoid within the fog but can't be sure. It was powerful, though. Very powerful."

She took a long sip of latte.

"But...we're all still alive. So that means something."

It did. I didn't like the idea of an archdemon running around my city, but could it really be worse than what we already had? With the undead in the slums and the necromancer controlling them...

I caught myself staring into the black of my coffee. So, did Cindy.

"So, I've told you about my recent failures, only fair that you share what you've been up to."

Where do I start? The vampires, the abductions, the mimic – or the necromancer. I've been busy...

"You know the undead," I said, avoiding eye contact. "They rise up, I cut them down."

I took a long drink of coffee to punctuate the statement.

Cindy snorted in amusement.

"Brett tells me you've been acting odd."

I raised my eyebrow. Brett said what?

"I don't think Brett knows me well enough to know what *odd* is for me."

Cindy laughed, but then leaned forward, serious. I noticed that the shaved part of her head had a small tattoo of a stylised sun on it. It was small. Her hair had been combed over it last time I saw her.

"I know about the vampires. I also know about what you didn't tell him in detail. About a voice on the telephone."

Her face was stern. Sterner than I'd ever seen it before, and I'd seen her lips and mouth caked in vomit from spell-sickness. This was a woman who sacrificed so much for her craft and mission. She drove herself to sickness to incant spells. Some, like Pranish's bastard older brother, would think her weak for that. I knew better. Cindy was strong. And she was staring me down.

"How...how did you find out?" I asked.

"I used to freelance for Conrad, you know?"

I did not. That explained it, though. Conrad was the only other person who knew about the necromancer on the phone.

"I know you were desperate, Kat, but you should know better than anyone not to make deals with necromancers."

"I didn't know they were a necromancer until it was too late. I haven't spoken to them since then."

That was true. The necromancer hadn't contacted me for months. Last call I'd had from them, they had said that, "this friendship had only just begun."

Ominous and stupid. I'd never be friends with a necromancer.

Cindy gestured at the waiter to bring another latte, and then turned back to me.

"I don't think you'd go dark on us, Kat, but best to be careful. Greater heroes than you have turned to villainy thinking they were doing the right thing. Don't get into bed with necromancers. I'd listen to Conrad on this, as much as I'd not listen to him on many other things. He has experience with making deals with the bad guys. He's learnt from his mistakes. At least, I hope so."

"Some people would say that Conrad is one of the bad guys," I said, trying to change the topic. Thoughts of the necromancer often sent shivers down my spine. There was not much else that could do that.

"Many people do think our dear old Conrad is a villain. Many people are also wrong. I know Conrad's face, and it isn't the face of evil. Evil is much vaguer. Harder to discern. All of Conrad's misbehaviour is out in the open. He is sincere about it. He is a scumbag, but he is, at his core, a good man," she said the last part almost reluctantly.

My coffee cup was empty. Cindy called the waiter to refill it without asking me.

"The Pinelands archdemon is not the first that I have faced," Cindy said, seemingly changing the topic. "Years ago, when I was still a hunter for Conrad, I was asked to investigate one of my fellow co-workers. A man who worked as Conrad's resident demonologist. Keep in mind that this was a different time. We don't understand a lot about demons now, but we knew even less back then. We didn't really understand the extent of corruption that studying demons could bring about. This man, who worked for Conrad, was named Pumpernickle."

I almost spat out my fresh coffee. Cindy was not amused.

"Not a name to inspire fear, I know. But, I soon learnt to fear the man."

She paused and drank her new latte.

"I hate rats," she continued, in almost a murmur. "Used to like them. Had two as pets when I was ten. But Pumpernickle kept rats. Had them crawling throughout his tweed coat. They spoke in tongues and Aramaic. He used to use them as spies. I found out later that they weren't just rats. He'd trapped lesser demons in rodents. I'm not sure how much you know about demons, Kat, but you must know that they never come to this world willingly. Seldom, do they ever come here willingly, at least. But, this man had ripped demons from their plain to put them in rats. Without their normal bodies, the demon-rats were easy to control for him. Yet, think of the audacity. He put a creature of pure primal energy and cardinal hatred, into the petite furry body of vermin."

"He sounds like a real piece of work."

"He was more than that. He was deranged. Completely and utterly. Conrad, to his credit, was too busy hiding from Goldfield spies to notice that Pumpernickle was murdering swathes of people to use in his rituals. When he did suspect something was wrong, he sent me after him. What I found made the pain of the scarring on my right-arm worth it."

She paused, contemplating her next words, while rubbing the scars on her arms.

"What are they for?" I asked, to keep the conversation flowing, while I gazed at the cursive-like scars across her right-arm. They looked like elvish from *Lord of the Rings*.

"This one is Turn Undead, as you saw at UCT. The other is a banishment spell."

My questioning look prompted her to explain.

"It allows me to channel my spark or the local weyline into driving a demon back to their realm – be it Hell, Raz'ed or the Damned Domains. The only thing that it requires is a name. A name, as we all know, is a vulnerability. For a demon, even more so."

I knew that much. Names were more than just an identifier on post-Cataclysmic Earth. They held a sense of true identity. With knowledge of a person's true name, you could hold power over them. You could target them with spells, mindwarp them and tether their souls to the world. True names were so important that most people had secret middle-names known by as few people as possible. I have one, and no, I'm not telling you.

"Pumpernickle had been acting strangely, according to Conrad. The Spell-Axe, the Brick, and myself, had all thought he'd always been odd, but Conrad believed something even more sinister was happening. He sent me to Pumpernickle's apartment. I found it abandoned. Not just abandoned recently, but for months. It was in a border slum, which explained why no one had noticed. As soon as I arrived, I could smell the rotting flesh. Pumpernickle was no necromancer. He didn't know how or care enough to stop the decay of his victims. He just left them there and used them to feed his rats. Well, he fed them what he didn't need. And for this, he needed a lot. Blood, limbs, skulls. Everything a demon of carnal violence may desire. Pumpernickle was used to brute-forcing demons. It's the typical way of summoning them. You trick them or force them into being summoned through sheer will. It works for lesser demons. For greater, like an archdemon, you need to make a deal. He made his deal. Fortunately, I was there to stop him."

"What was the deal?"

"He offered blood, sacrifice, death and destruction, and his body from which to do it. He brought an archdemon into this world and sacrificed himself to do it. But he made one error. He didn't know I was present and didn't think I'd have recognised the prominent archdemon he was in the process of summoning. I spoke its name, while engraving this spell into my arm and my memory. By doing so, I avoided risking it possessing me as well. The archdemon was banished for my efforts."

I hadn't touched my coffee. When it was clear she had stopped speaking, I asked.

"Why? Why did he do it?"

I understood summoning demons to feed one of the cardinal sins. To sate one's greed, lust for vengeance, to gain power — but what could drive a man to sacrifice his own life to bring evil into the world?

"I don't know, Kat. And I don't want to know. Those who try to understand evil can't help but become a little evil themselves."

I frowned. What did that mean for me? I had faced evil so many times before. I liked to think I understood it.

"Pumpernickle is dead," Cindy finally said. "And that's that. He is my rival, to a degree. He is dead, but we are still fighting. Every demon is his work. A symbol of his maniacal goals. After I put him and his archdemon down, I left Conrad and became a full-time purifier, and now a part-time healer."

Both our second drinks were done. Cindy was silent. She was still holding onto the glass mug that had contained her latte. Her index fingernails were painted black and white.

"Why did you tell me all this?" I finally asked.

"Don't make deals with devils. Devils of all types, Kat," Cindy whispered, hushed, but filled with power. "Evil is evil. Evil used for good is just as evil. I know you were desperate to save Trudie, but next time, do not converse with the darkness."

Did I have a choice?

Could I have left my friend to die? But even then, was saving her worth it?

I didn't know, and I don't think there is a good answer.

Cindy stood, suddenly.

"I'll pay for the coffee," she said.

I made a motion to argue but she stopped me.

"I was also a student once. It is the role of the ex-student to alleviate the current student's plight."

She gave me a faint smile. I gave her my thanks.

She paid the bill and made a move to leave. I did the same. Needed to get home to make sure Duer wasn't growing any toadstools. He was likable enough, but pixies had a particularly mischievous nature. Couldn't blame them for it but couldn't let them run amok either. Then, I remembered something.

"Cindy…"

She stopped and turned.

"When I was on the island…" I began. How should I continue? How could I explain it to her? I didn't know what I had done myself.

"When I was on the island, with the vampires, I said something that made whatever the vampires were summoning retreat."

Cindy raised an eyebrow.

"I've read LeBlanc's new book on the Ancient Theory. Brett described something that matches LeBlanc's description."

The fact that she heard these things from Brett made me slightly irritated, and a bit jealous. That last part made me even more irritated.

I hid my annoyance and nodded. "It tried to bite me, to turn me into a true vampire, I think, but I managed to resist. I said something to it and it recoiled. I don't know what it was I said though, or how…"

I swallowed my words. I didn't know what else to say. That time was a blur. I couldn't even recount what I had said. All I knew is that I had said something, and that I wasn't a drained corpse or forced into vampire servitude.

Cindy turned to face me fully. She was wearing her full Heiligeslicht regalia and looked mighty respectable, if a bit intimidating.

"Magic is the language of nature," she said, simply. "Contrary to popular belief, humans are also a part of nature. Within many of us exist the words needed to bring light against the dark. For most of us, we cannot bring it out without intense study. Even sorcerers like myself need to embrace wizardry to channel purification incantations. But, even then, there are words that are anathema to evil. Try to remember them, Kat. They may come to be useful to you again."

She turned, then murmured, "They may come to help us all, in the end."

Chapter 7. Demonology

I don't know if it was my conversation with Cindy that sparked a new-found interest, but I started looking into demons. Not deeply. As Cindy said, demonologists had a penchant for being corrupted, but just enough to attempt to sate my voracious curiosity.

"You should be looking up on the undead," Treth said. "They're our *raison d'etre.*"

He had learnt the French term and was using it any chance he got.

"Variety is the spice of life," I responded, paging through some demonic cosmology on my phone while waiting for Trudie to finish her class. We were going out to buy some music. She was into some new goth darkwave stuff and I couldn't help but also enjoy it. It usually had a sick beat and twisted enough lyrics to appeal to my inner demons.

"But focus is the meat," Treth responded.

"Touché," I said, using another French term. It was a day for French, it seems, despite my Scottish, Irish, Rhodesian and South African heritage. "But, can't hurt to look into demons a bit. We may just fight one someday.

We know enough about the undead already. Time to expand our horizons like we did with spirits."

"Can never know enough…"

"Exactly, so I'm learning about demons."

And there was a lot to learn. After music shopping with Trudie, who found my constant reading of demonic lore irritating, I continued my research in earnest at home. Duer was particularly worried for me, but I satisfied him with vodka and honey. Pixies are easy to understand, unlike demons.

In my studies, what I found particularly interesting was how accurate pre-Cataclysmic demonologists actually were with their studies. While the crackpots of Earth, before magic actually became a thing, were usually just that – crackpots – a lot of the demonic cosmology written down by Medieval, Enlightenment and modern-day scholars ended up being closer to the truth than expected.

Plenty of the demons of myth that haunted human nightmare and scary bedtime stories ended up being real. Krampus, the horned goat-demon who punished children around Christmas time, for instance. He was contained by a cult of central European demon-catchers twenty years ago. Lucky for the demon-catchers, he wasn't a powerful demon. He had entered Earth willingly to enact his weird agenda. He wasn't exactly angry about being captured. He just wondered what took the humans so long.

Other demons were not as pleasant.

Demons, in essence, are the carnal and primal left-overs of creation. While spirits are the left-overs of the now departed living, demons are the left-overs of the beginning. Not just of the beginning of it all, while some are by-products of just that, but the beginning of all things. Every strong idea, emotion, event, invention…may breed a demon. While some demons are very simple in illustrating this, like the elemental djinns who embody the forces of fire, earth, air and water, others are much more complex. The archdemons of the originally Christian mythos are a good example. They embody the essences of particular traits. These traits often being seen as the cardinal sins, of course. There was Lucifer of Pride, and Satan of Wrath, of course, but there were others. Mammon of Greed, Asmodeus of Lust. Leviathan of Envy. Beelzebub of Gluttony and Belphegor of Sloth.

There were many more archdemons, but these were particularly pertinent to a society that used to be dominated by Christianity. After the Cataclysm, when the truth of these demons was revealed, but the veracity of the religion as a whole was not, there was a lot of chaos in the Church. Over the years, organised religion shrank and shrank. It returned to the days before the rise of the Catholic church. There were no mega religions any more. Just a lot of cults – some holding onto past favour.

What I wanted to know, however, was the nature of these archdemons' names. Names were a vulnerability, as Cindy told me, so how did such powerful beings let their true names be known by mere mortals? Or were they their true names at all? Were we holding onto the false names of demons in a vain hope to banish them? When the real battle came, would we attempt to banish such a demon and be laughed at for our troubles?

More pertinently: who was the archdemon that appeared in Pinelands? Was it one of the seven archdemons of the Christian cosmology, rulers of the hosts of Hell, or was it one of the bestial demons of Raz'ed? Perhaps, even, one of the amorphous terrors from the Damned Worlds.

The problem with demons and identifying them was that there were so many types. And for many, you could not even classify them as types. All that held them together as demons was that ever vague definition, essence of creation.

They were like nothing I had ever studied before. They were physical, yet not exactly organic. They were an essence, yet not incorporeal. They were bound to rules, but nobody had the rulebook.

They fascinated me, and I was glad that Conrad reminded me that I had night-shift at the Citadel, for the more I felt myself absorbed by the study of demons, the more I understood Cindy's words. One could not stop with mere study of demons. Eventually, one would want to make a deal with the devil. If only for more knowledge...

***

It was dark on top of Table Mountain. Only the few lights of the cable station and the distant aura of Hope City and Old Town lit up the silhouette of the Citadel. I had only a few square meters of eerie white light and the small beam of my flashlight to guide my patrol around the Titan Citadel.

Not every monster was around day and night. Some could only appear in one or the other. While I had gathered no leads during the day, that didn't mean there wasn't something I could find at night.

93

I rubbed my shoulders in the chilly night air. I had my full ensemble of gear on, leather jacket, scratchy bite-proof scarf, face-plate and even an extra jersey underneath it all. All of that couldn't stop the wind and the nip in the air.

"I never thought I'd be thankful for dilapidated buildings," I said, through chattering teeth. It was directed at Treth but said to fill the silence.

"How come?" he replied. His voice sounded wary. He was watching our flanks, ensuring nothing could sneak up on us.

"Fewer angles of attack. And less wind."

Treth grunted his assent.

I didn't think I'd find anything out at night. The door to the Citadel was lined with silver. A night spirit wouldn't be able to enter. There were beasts that didn't mind silver, however. Plenty of undead (my bread and butter) and quite a few living fiends. But in a world constantly changing with all sorts of different types of monsters, it was hard to nail down what could be responsible for anything. It'd really help if Stephen could grow up and give me access to the surveillance footage. Then I wouldn't have to be traipsing around all night for a pay check like some wage-slave. Sure, a healthy and stable income is good, but I prefer hustling.

There is an unbeatable independence and dignity in working for oneself. Every inch of success is earned with grit and blood. And if I've learnt anything in my line of work: suffering is often virtue.

I'd be glad when I was shot of this case. It was interesting finally visiting the Titan Citadel, but I wouldn't miss it once I was gone.

I sighed and sat down on a flat-topped rock by the stone path. My flashlight attached to my bag strap shook and flickered from the sudden vibrations.

"Nothing. Absolutely nothing. I'm starting to think one of the mages is killing their own at this rate."

I snorted. That was ridiculous. The sorcerers who powered the Citadel were loyal to the point of fanaticism. The Cult existed for a reason – they needed unfailing loyalty to the cause.

I felt Treth hesitate. "Buck up, soldier."

I couldn't help but laugh at the forced sheepishness in his voice.

"What?" he asked, incredulous.

"Buck up? Another phrase you've picked up?"

Silence, and a tinge of embarrassment from the knightly spirit. I stopped laughing, and felt a sombre air descend over us, contrasting with the damned gale hitting my back.

"You used to give a lot more sage wisdom," I murmured, while I fidgeted with the pommel of my sheathed dusack.

"You used to need it."

"That a compliment, Mr Concord?"

"I'm from Concord, not Mr Concord."

"That a compliment, man from Concord?"

More hesitation. What was Treth thinking in his non-physical mind? What thoughts were going through the head of this alien who I felt so close to, by choice and by design? Would I ever know? And should I?

"You don't need compliments, Kat."

I leaned back and gazed at the night sky. It was a clear evening, and the stars were in abundance.

"Your sage wisdom got me this far, Treth. Need it or not, I kinda…miss it."

Silence. Why was he being so coy? He used to be a knight paladin who killed powerful undead, for Rifts' sake! We should be comfortable enough with each other to get a bit personal. Well, I can't blame him completely. I'm a closed book, and I haven't been forthcoming with him in the past. In that regard, we are both very similar.

The pause became silence and I gritted my teeth.

"Treth..."

"Kat, there's a light."

I stopped and looked around. Treth was right. In the distance, floating like a wisp in the wind, was a little orange flame, emerging from the black.

"Nobody but Titan mages and myself are meant to be up here," I said.

"So, seems we have our lead. Go."

I stood up, drew my swords, and entered the blackness away from the shallow pool of light being cast by the cable station.

"Turn off the flashlight," Treth whispered, even though only I could hear him.

I did. While many monsters had night-vision, it was still best to attune my own vision to the dark. The moon would be all the source of light I'd need.

The orange speck became a more pronounced flame as I came closer and closer. My boots, an upgrade over my usual sneakers, crunched on organic debris and fynbos. Couldn't be helped. The flame didn't move, however. It remained, until the moon seemed to brighten, and I arrived at the foot of a boulder. Atop it sat a suit-wearing man with short, black hair, a hawklike nose, pale skin and a pair of black horns protruding from his scalp like a deer's. In his hand, he held a lit pipe as long as my forearm. He held it delicately, as if it was a flower, but did not lift it to his lips.

He paid no heed to my presence, but I knew that he had noticed me a long time ago. He sat with his legs dangling over the edge of the boulder, assured that he would not hurt himself. There was a confidence in his posture, yet also an immense sadness.

I opened my mouth to speak. Stopped, and then started again, as sternly as I could.

"Who are you? What are you doing here?"

He did not look at me as he spoke. Rather, he looked out into the distance, over Hope City and its undying lights.

"So much has changed," he said, simply. His voice was…normal. I don't know how to describe it. It was neither too deep nor too sharp. It was not a voice for radio, but it wasn't a voice that would be too bad on radio either. It was perfectly average, and that is what somehow made it unique.

"Answer me, creature," I said, loudly. It was the way I spoke to the more intelligent undead when I meant to unnerve them. Wights rose to challenges very easily. Taunting them threw them off guard. But this man just continued sitting. Staring.

"I sat near this rock…I don't know how long ago," he continued. "I still smoked back then. It was still considered a temptation. Something to be proud of. A competition, rather than a silly vice. I meant to be the best at it. And I expected to be."

I raised my eyebrow. Best at smoking?

"I would gaze out from this rock. It was a very different place back then. Man was only just settling. No skyscrapers. No lights. Just a few settler shanties and ranches. I'd say I miss it, but then I would be lying. There was a charm, but progress is something to accept."

The man shrugged.

"But there is something I miss." He sighed. "The man who bested me…"

He laughed, short and bittersweet.

"We covered this mountain in a fog so thick that people called it the tablecloth. We smoked and smoked. Him, to stay away from his wife. Me, because it was something to do."

The man raised the pipe closer to his lips, and then stopped.

"He bested me, that man whose name I cannot recall despite my best efforts. He bested me and outlasted me. And I cursed him for it..."

He stopped and gazed once more onto the city.

I stepped closer, tightening my grip on my swords.

"Careful, Kat," Treth warned, and I felt a very real fear in his voice.

"Did you..." I began. Swallowed. "Did you kill the mages?"

Silence.

And then.

"Yes."

Instinct overwhelmed fear, as it often did in me, and I jumped towards the man. His legs dangled so that I could probably get in a decent swipe to wound him, and then drag him down to finish him off.

That is if I hadn't been shot back five metres with a bleeding nose and an instant headache. I shook the ringing out of my head and jumped back up. The man stood before me. Half a metre away. His arms were behind his back, still holding the pipe.

With a roar, I slashed in an upward arc with my left sword. Treth roared with me. He clicked his fingers without looking at us. We both stopped suddenly as we felt the pain. I had never been shocked by electricity, but I imagined this was what it felt like. I recoiled and looked at my arm. It was fine. I could move it. But my sword was shattered to the hilt. It didn't look scorched or bent. It was just as if the metal above the hilt had been deleted.

"There is a right way to do things, Kat Drummond," the man said, simply.

I looked at him. He looked so human, if not for the pitch-black horns. But despite his humanness, my chest tensed, my breathing stopped, and my heart hurt. I felt a very real terror. He returned to his seat in a blink, twiddling the pipe in his hands. He looked at me and I felt tears rise to my eyes. All I could think about was one thing: run. Yet, my body could not move. I held impotently onto the hilt of my broken sword.

He shook his head.

"Go."

My body didn't need further prompting. I dropped my broken sword and ran the way I had come, towards the dark silhouette of the Citadel, and the cable station at its base. My heart raced faster than I. Raced faster than I thought prudent.

I'd fought wights, vampires, spirits, monsters and hordes of undead. I'd faced down terror made manifest. Why then did facing this simple looking horned man fill me with such terror.

"Kat!" Treth yelled at me.

I was breathing too fast. I knew it, but there wasn't much I could do about it. A panicked person doesn't tend to care about the rational voice in their head telling them to calm down.

"Kat, snap out of it. We have to get out of here," Treth yelled again, sounding fearful himself. He'd been anxious in the past – Treth was a nervy guy – but I'd never heard this much terror in his voice. It only drove me further into the abyss. That dark, chaotic chasm of fear and animalistic terror, where only instinct rules and one would throw themselves off a cliff to make it stop.

102

The small voice in my head, not Treth's, told me to get a grip. To realise that this terror was unfounded. That I'd just get a new sword. The man-creature had told me to go. He didn't mean to give chase. But then why did my heart threaten to beat out of my chest and run away itself?

"Get up, Kat," Treth said, pleadingly.

My eyes had already been open, but I truly opened them. I was on all fours, puking my guts out onto the bushes that I'd fallen onto. I retched, and retched, until there was nothing left.

"Get to the station. We need to regroup."

Treth was remaining calm, even though I knew he was also terrified. I lifted myself up and felt the wind chill the sweat on my back.

"Where?" I asked, meekly. Where was the cable station? I had run towards the Citadel. At least, what I thought was the Citadel. But no lights were on. My flash light, I now noticed, had been destroyed by whatever wave of force had shattered my sword. I was in the dark. Only the moonlight, the distant city lights and the still flickering pipe in the distance.

"I…don't know…" Treth finally answered.

"The lights were on earlier, right?" I still had a stammer to my voice but was slowly trying to regain my composure.

Come on, Kat. You've been through so much worse.

But I wasn't sure that I had. Not really. There was a menace around that creature that I couldn't put my finger on but felt more intense than anything I'd ever faced before.

"Did we go in the wrong direction?" I asked.

"No, I don't think so... There is the Citadel, I think. That small red light is the camera."

"Then the cable station should be near it. And it was lit up earlier."

I froze in place and felt a shiver go up my spine. The cable station's lights were off. Which meant the security wasn't there? Which meant I wouldn't be able to get off the mountain.

"Kat, calm down."

"I am calm!" I lied, my heart racing.

Stuck on the mountain. In the dark. With that...thing.

Oh, Rifts. I'd need a raise after this.

That's not what I cared about right now, though. All I wanted was to get as far from that creature as possible.

I headed to the red light and found that Treth was correct. I felt for the doorbell and rang it.

Nothing.

I rang it again. And knocked the door with the pommel of my sword.

Nothing.

"Fuck…"

I felt moisture in my eyes. I just wanted to get back to my apartment. To my bed. To Alex. To Duer. I wanted to phone Trudie and hear her voice. To talk about the albums we'd bought earlier today. Anything to distract me from what I'd experienced.

"Follow the path, Kat. See if the station is still manned."

I heard the doubt in his voice. He knew what I knew. The station was abandoned. The bastard on duty had clocked out early. I'd make sure he lost his head because of it.

The lack of reply when I banged on the door and shouted only added to my angst. I was alone. Well, we were alone. Me, Treth and the man-creature with the pipe.

I rubbed my shoulders. My surviving sword had been sheathed a while ago. It had already been proven ineffective. That thought stung. A lot. Stung more than the chill. My jacket wasn't enough for this night air. The cold fear and sweat made it worse.

The Citadel wasn't letting me in. The cable station was closed. There was a monster far surpassing my abilities on the peak with me and the night was only getting colder.

My lip quivered in a way that shamed me, but I stopped the moisture in my eyes from collecting any further.

I pounded on the cable station door one more time and then slumped to the floor.

"What do I do, Treth?" I asked, a quaver to my voice. I trembled. Half from cold, half from fearful desperation.

"Find shelter," he said. "Get out of the wind."

I didn't expect him to say it. It came out so naturally. As if Treth had been a camper in his life. He may have been, for all I knew. Treth didn't talk about his life that much. All I knew was that he'd been a paladin in an order of undead hunters and had been killed by his own brother who had become a lich. Sounds like a lot but trust me. It wasn't much. Treth and I were pretty private. All he knew about me was that I'd watched my parents be sacrificed for a necromantic ritual. So, not much.

I stood up.

"What do I look for?"

I really didn't know. I'm a city-dweller. The top of Table Mountain is effectively wilderness. I was out of my element.

"Go towards the dark silhouettes. Those small hills, over there. I think I saw some small caves when we were patrolling during the day."

I took one step and stopped.

"Fuck, Treth. I have a class in the morning. I should be in bed. Maybe Trudie is right. I should stop doing this. Should try to be...normal."

"I know, Kat," he said, soothingly and very much out of character. "But we're here now. Can't change that now. We'll see if you want to be normal when we're warmer and safer."

I nodded and went forward. One step at a time.

Eventually, I found a cave in the darkness. The small twinkle of my lighter illuminated it. It looked safe enough, and even had some dead and dry foliage inside to light, for some temporary warmth. We didn't worry about the creature. If he wanted us dead, we'd be dead. For whatever reason, he let us live. That was somehow scarier than the necromancers and zombies who kept trying to kill me. I crawled into the opening, hit my head on the rock ceiling, recovered, and then lit the kindling. The light and warmth were a short but worthy blessing. It killed most of the chill. I curled up near the embers as it was extinguished. There were no better pieces of wood outside to make a more sustainable fire, and I didn't want to go out again. This would need to be warm enough.

The rock floor was sandy, and I had only my hard backpack as a pillow. I held my knees with my arms, my hands in either sleeve to keep them warm.

Wasn't the most pleasant experience I've had.

"Worst hunt?" I asked.

"Can't be worse than the mimic," Treth said.

I snorted. I'd been swallowed by the shapeshifting beast while wearing a new dress for a date. A white dress, I might add. It was red when I was done with the creature.

"At least we killed that monster. This thing…"

"Hmmm…"

"What is it?" I whispered.

"I…don't know."

"A demon, I think."

I felt Treth's assent.

"Pretty poetic. I was studying them this afternoon, realising how little I knew, and then…we face one here."

"Poetic indeed. As if it was foreshadowed."

"It looked very human."

I felt Treth's agreement again, and his fear. He felt what I felt. It was that eerie humanness that made the creature so much scarier. It wasn't merely uncanny. It didn't look like it was imitating humanity or was even a deformed human – like a mutant or zombie. It looked exactly human. Living, breathing. If not for the horns, I would have thought I was facing a sorcerer.

It was more than the horns, though. There was an air of intense…evil? No, not that. But it was scary. Too scary to just be a human with fake horns. It was a creature not of this world. I knew that much.

Treth must have felt my anxiety pick up, as he spoke, in that soothing voice I was not used to from him. He was my drill instructor, my mentor, and my comrade…but he'd never really comforted me. Just shouted at me until I got back up.

"I haven't been in a cave like this for…I don't know how long."

"I thought you lived in a church, or some sort of castle."

"I did…near the end."

There was something I recognised. That hesitation in his voice. Not just the hesitation to tell me, I sensed, but the reluctance to recall it at all.

I closed my eyes. To attempt to sleep, but also to show Treth that he didn't need to open any shut doors. He could keep his secrets, like I did mine. Our demons, not like the one with his pipe, belonged behind locked doors.

Treth sighed. Heavily, exasperated.

"You don't need to tell me, Treth," I murmured, cheek pressed up against the bag.

"I…know. But, I want to."

I went silent and let him speak. He was quiet too, then spoke, after what seemed an eternity.

"My brother and I grew up poor. Street urchins. Products of a war between lords who were enemies one season and feasting buddies the next. My family had a smallholding, once, but when our father was pressed into the poor fucking infantry and my mother was raped and killed by soldiers from our side or the other, whatever that means, my brother and I fled. Orphans, for all intents and purposes. We never found out what happened to our dad, but we kinda knew. Pikemen don't live that long. They hold the line without any armour or shield. Only a long piece of sharpened wood, meant to stop a charge of metal and hooves…"

There was a strain in his voice that hurt me, deeply.

"Treth…"

He ignored me and continued.

"We lived in caves like this for ages afterwards. We lived in different lords' lands, never stopping for more than a day. We poached fish and animals. Lost food to rangers, bandits and bigger predators more often than not. But, we got better. We got used to it. The caves stopped being cold and dank. They became home. A different home every day, but somehow the same. It was our place to be safe. We became better at finding food. We stopped eating the berries that gave us the runs and learnt how to trap the bears that kept stealing our salmon. We even got on the good side of some rangers, who turned a blind eye to our poaching. Ages passed, and I even came to enjoy the life we had."

He paused, and I felt him look around this small, stony shelter. What did he see in this blackness that I did not?

Was he alone, with me or with another? Would I ever know?

"That all changed, as things often do. We were pushed out of the greens, the forests and the plains. A rot came to the land, heralding a darkness that forced us peasant and hunter-gathering folk into the cities."

"The undead?" I asked, hushed. Treth's silence was confirmation enough.

"The cities were safe from the necromancers and undead, but they weren't safe from other things. Gangs ruled. The local lords and nobles were barely distinguishable from them. My brother...protected me."

I knew why Treth hesitated. His brother had become a lich, a powerful undead necromancer, and then slain him. Treth lived in permanent guilt that he had not killed his own brother. I didn't blame him.

Treth must have read my thoughts about his brother.

"Alain wasn't always the evil that sent my spirit reeling across worlds. He loved me, and I loved him. If not, then I would have been able to kill him. I would have been able to recognise his evil and put him in the dirt where he belonged..."

"He was your brother, Treth."

"Yes… He was…And he had been there for me on the streets of Gazore. Those dark, stinking streets. Worse than the slums here."

"We've never been to the true slums."

"The border slums then, but it was an unceasing darkness for us. Food was harder to come by. Can't just catch a rabbit. Best we could do in the city was catch rats. And that's if we could find one that hadn't been caught by someone else first. One night, my brother came home with meat and I almost refused to eat it. I didn't know where or how he'd got it. But I was so hungry. I still don't know where it was from, and I don't want to know. What matters is that Alain kept me safe, but in his desire to keep me safe, he fell in with a bad crowd. A street gang. I joined them as well…"

He stopped.

"What happened next?" I pressed. He had my curiosity now, and while I know that I should not press a man talking about painful memories, I was never one for tenderness. Plus, Treth is kind of a part of me. I felt that I needed to know.

"Alain pushed me to do worse and worse things. Theft, vandalism, murder. But, one day I tried to rob a man armoured in white and gold. He caught me and brought me to his chapel. He became my master. Sir Arden of Drambyre, Knight-Paladin of the Order of Albin. He indentured me to his service as a page, and then a squire...and then a knight. Alain disappeared, and I couldn't find him. But, I did not want to. The Order taught me discipline, respect, and gave me a home with principles that I could be proud of. When I met Alain again, he was no longer truly alive. I couldn't believe my eyes, and felt an overwhelming guilt that if I had tried to find him, he could have embraced the light like me..."

There was almost a desperate sob in the last sentence. I didn't press again. Treth was a proud man. I shouldn't make him cry.

Treth remained silent.

"Thank you, Treth."

"For what?"

"For telling me...this. We've been together for so long, but we don't know all that much about each other. We're closed books, you and I, but maybe it's time we're more open."

Treth nodded. "Learn from my mistakes, Kat."

"Mistakes?"

"Evil isn't always rotting. It can be something you love. Something you loved. But it is evil all the same."

I imagined the demon with the pipe. He had sad eyes, in an attractive face. Without the horns, he would be someone I'd find appealing.

But he was evil. He had to be. And while I may have failed, I felt charging him was the right thing to do.

"You have an early class tomorrow, Kat. Get some sleep. I'll keep watch."

"Thanks, Treth…" I yawned. "Thanks…for…being there…"

Despite the rocky floor below, darkness took me, and I drifted into the land of sleep.

I dreamt of castles, of hunting animals and of death. A lot of death.

Chapter 8. Cranky

I awoke to a sea of green, mingling between bulwarks of solid grey rock. A thin layer of moisture adhered to it all, reflecting the morning sun. I heard running water. It had rained in the night, forming thin rivulets of moisture on smoothed rocks. I hoped that meant clean water. My throat felt like an ashtray. There was a pleasant smell, at least, as the wet soil emitted a clean aroma across the land. It leant a freshness to the air.

"Good morning, Kat," Treth said. He didn't sound like he had been awake all night. To my knowledge, he never slept. He didn't need to. He had no body to get tired.

I let out a yawn, lifted myself up, and then swore loudly as I hit my head on the roof of my rock shelter.

"A good shitty morning to you too, Treth," I said, through gritted teeth. I felt a wave of amusement emanate from my incorporeal companion.

"Nothing assailed you in your sleep. Nothing that I can detect, at least," he said.

"I guessed so. I'd hope you'd wake me up if something was to *assail* me."

"A little bit cranky this morning?" I imagined a juvenile grin on his face.

"A little bit inappropriately joyful?" I retorted. He did have an irritating hint of cheer to his voice.

"Not all memories of my life are unpleasant. This smell…it reminds me of the good times."

I couldn't empathise with his nostalgic joy, as I pulled myself out from the little cave where I'd spent the night. My everything ached.

I was alive, at least. I'd survived the night on top of a mountain with a monster I was really not sure I could slay. I still felt like shit, though.

I retrieved my backpack, squashed by my head during the night. There was a flask inside. The coffee would be cold now, but cold coffee was better than no coffee. But the flask was empty.

I raised an incredulous eyebrow.

"Treth, did I drink any coffee while I slept?"

He thought for a second. "No, and I can't recall you drinking any of it last night."

I tipped the flask over for good measure. Nothing. Dry as the northern, ogre-infested desert. I didn't want to think about how it had got that way. I guessed it had something to do with that demon. When he had done whatever had destroyed my sword, it might have also dissipated my beverage.

That was last night, though. It was now today. And I was very thirsty.

"It rained last night," Treth said. "Must be some place where the water was caught."

After some searching, I found a small little rock bowl, indented into the surface of a boulder submerged into the fynbos-covered soil. A good amount of water had collected in the bowl, mingling with the dirt.

I stuck my nose up at it. I was a city slicker, after all. Never camped. Never left the city. My idea of roughing it was staking out an abandoned building, not drinking water out of a dirty pool.

Treth laughed. "It won't kill you, Kat. Drink it. Better than anything out of a bottle."

I bent down to collect some with the cup of my flask.

"Too much city, Kat. Drink with your hands. Feel the water. The minerals…"

I rolled my eyes but did so. The water was refreshingly cool on my hands, lips and throat. Despite a little bit of dirt, it might as well have been the best thing I'd ever tasted. Don't knock true thirst's ability to make things seem nicer than they are. After I had quenched my thirst, I splashed water on my face. That woke me up and got rid of a lot of my morning crankiness. Not all of it though. I had enough to throw at the people who'd kept me on this mountain all night.

After that, I took care of private matters and made my way towards the Citadel. It was a shimmering black behemoth as the morning damp clung to it like a thin waterfall on a rockface. Along the way to the Citadel, I was side-tracked by thin sparkles of light in the bushes.

My sword. Well, what was left of it. I touched the blade. They were cool, wet from the rain and shattered into irreparable little bits.

"You served me well. Now it's just gonna be your brother from now on."

"Going to bury it?" Treth chided.

"Shut up, Treth," I said, unable to hide a bit of sadness. Maybe the blade shards did deserve a burial...

I stood up and looked at the rock where the demon had been sitting last night. It was empty now. Didn't expect him to still be here. But I did expect there to be some other sign of him. Pipe ash, litter, or at least footprints. But the only footprints and damaged shrubbery

I could find were from me. Only my broken blade served to confirm that what had happened last night was not just my imagination.

I sighed. "Got some time till class. Enough time to give the Citadel hell for locking me up here."

"Go easy on them."

"No."

Unlike last night, the door to the Citadel opened after one ring. I entered to the sight of a shocked Cornelius.

"What the fuck happened last night?" I yelled, and immediately regretted as the man's eyes widened like a deer facing down a werewolf.

"I...uh...what...?" he stuttered.

Maybe I should go easy on him? He gets enough shit from DuPreez.

"I was locked up here last night with a fucking demon. Rang the doorbell fifty billion times and got no answer. This how you treat your employees?"

I'm not one for sensitivity.

"There...there was a lockdown last night...Kat," he stuttered out, leaning back on his desk to support himself. My guilt at shouting at him and my anger at what I'd gone through was evenly matched and vying for dominance. "Demon...?"

"A demon...yeah..." I contemplated swearing again. I let out a heavy sigh instead.

"I'm sorry, Cornelius. Just...had a bad night."

"Did you sleep on the mountain?"

I glared at him, then nodded.

"What about the cable station?"

"Closed. Not a soul in sight."

He approached me and tentatively put his hand on my shoulder. My glare didn't put him off, so I gave up. I just hoped I could keep up my anger. Didn't want to burst out crying.

"I'll find out who was supposed to be on duty last night. Will get him fired."

"Yeah," I replied, simply. "Thanks."

"What's all this racket?" DuPreez rumbled, entering the reception area.

Cornelius stiffened. I responded before Cornelius found it necessary to do so.

"I've got a lead, Mr DePreez."

"A lead? Mind enlightening me?"

I waved away the request. I didn't feel like telling this man anything in my current mood.

"I'll let you know through the appropriate channels at the appropriate time. For now, I must be getting to class."

I left the building before DuPreez could respond.

"You sure know how to make friends," Treth said.

I grunted in response. Didn't need more friends. Had a good bunch already. And why would I want to be friends with DuPreez? Well, I should have been nicer to Cornelius. Not his fault I was locked out.

I channelled my residual anger into glares at the Whiteshield guards on duty at the top and bottom cable stations. At least the taxi got to the bottom station before I lost control and started shouting at the guards.

I was cutting it fine to get to class. Was one of those less forgiving schedules today. Would need to drop my bags off at the Gravekeeper, it was en route, and then head straight to campus. No time to shower. As usual...

***

Class was revision. Could have skipped it and showered instead. Would have been much more productive. Instead, I held my head up and tried to keep my eyes open as the professor went on about Titan mages and lawmancers. I

122

was fortunate to be too tired to shout out. I was sick of damn Titan mages! Sick of them and the demon hunting them. I'd just been studying demons yesterday, and then one pops out and almost kills me. Last part was a lie, though, I felt. I'm sure that if that thing wanted me dead, I'd be dead. The sword was a show of power. The demon wanted me to know what it was capable of, I thought. But then there was all that weird stuff it was talking about. It sounded like it missed someone. All very peculiar, and as I was wrapping my head around it, I was pulled out of my reverie by the shuffling of students. The class had ended. I followed the mob like a zombie and was greeted by the almost vampiric visage of Trudie.

"Hey," she said. "Your cell was going to voice mail last night, but Andy said he saw you arrive on campus."

I gave her a hug. She returned it.

"You look terrible." She sniffed. "And smell terrible, but not as bad as usual. What were you doing last night?"

I clung on, almost leaning on her for support. She was shorter than me and made a nice arm and headrest. I put almost all my weight on her, giving her a bit of punishment for the rude comment.

"Camping," I muttered. She snorted. Didn't believe me.

I let go of my friend and checked my phone. The screen was black. I tried to press it on. No dice.

"You need to keep it charged," Trudie said.

"I'm not that technologically inept," I grunted, fiddling with the device. In fact, I wasn't technologically inept at all. I had helped Trudie with a lot of her computer stuff in the past.

Trudie snatched the cell out of my hand and reached into her pocket, revealing a cable linked up to a power bank. She plugged it in and tried to switch it on. Still didn't work.

"What did you do to it?" she muttered, squinting at the dead device.

"I didn't do anything…"

But a certain demon might have…

"Kat break her phone?" Andy said, appearing behind me. I almost jumped. Almost.

He walked to Trudie's side and put his arm around her shoulders. I raised my eyebrow at that. Especially seeing that she didn't flinch or even notice. She was too busy fiddling with my very dead cell phone.

"I'll take a look at it, Kat," she said. "But until then…"

She revealed a small cell from her pocket. "I've got a spare."

I accepted it. No point arguing. Trudie would expect it back after she had sorted out my cell. If it could be sorted out. Trudie opened up the back of the cell and took out its SIM card. I took it and inserted it into the new cell. I hoped the SIM was okay. Didn't want to have to get a new number. At least I could easily download and log into the MonsterSlayer app. Couldn't be without my bread and butter.

"So, where did you camp last night?" Andy asked, arm still around Trudie's shoulder.

"Table Mountain," I muttered, reluctantly. I'm not good at hiding my feelings. And my feelings towards Andy right now were irritation, resentment and a peculiar jealousy.

"Table Mountain? Didn't take you for a Titan Pilgrim."

"I'm not…"

I looked around for an escape route. Didn't find any but didn't let that stop me.

"Anyway, I gotta go."

I turned and walked away as fast as I could.

"Kat!" I heard Trudie call, once I was quite a bit away. I winced but stopped. She caught up with me, which must have been hard. She was wearing heels while I was wearing boots.

"What the hell was that, Kat?" Trudie spat.

I almost sniggered at the rhyme but collected myself.

"What was what? I needed to go. I have to look into this case…"

"You know what's what. You've been treating Andy like shit recently. You and Pranish, but at least Pranish can pretend to be nice. What the fuck is going on?"

I sighed. I'd told Trudie my reasoning before. She didn't agree with me. Andy had not helped find her when she'd been kidnapped by vampires. Trudie thought he'd done nothing wrong. That he couldn't be blamed for having a life. I thought differently. If you didn't risk something to save a friend, they weren't really your friend.

Trudie rolled her eyes and continued speaking before I could say anything.

"Whatever's got you acting like this, cut it. As you might have guessed, Andy and I are seeing each other now…"

"That escalated quickly," I tried to make it sound like a joke, but it came out sounding serious.

"You are hardly around, Kat. Things happen when you aren't in the room."

She frowned.

"I know you dated a bit. My fault, really, but we've really hit it off recently. He's a good guy, even if you don't think so. So, please be nice. For my sake."

I nodded, slowly. Trudie took that as assent.

"Thanks. I've got a class now. Will hit you up when I've got the cell fixed."

I waved her off and turned.

Trudie and Andy. Dating. I didn't know what to think about that.

Chapter 9. Archives

I put Trudie's loaned phone to good use and phoned Cindy while taking a seat on a bench near Jammie Plaza. It was a lot more peaceful than a few months ago, when the necromancer, Jeramiah Cox, released a horde of undead onto my campus to punish me for breaking up his twisted plan to cure terminal illness and bring about socialised healthcare through turning everyone into zombies. There was a memorial set up in the middle of the plaza to commemorate those who had died. I tried not to look at it. I felt more than a bit responsible for their deaths.

"Hey, Kat. What's up?" Cindy answered. The SIM still worked, and my number was now assigned to this new phone.

"Met a demon last night."

"Fun."

I heard a faint hum, a hiss and then a burst, like a fluorescent bulb bursting. Cindy swore, put down the phone and then picked it up again.

"I hope this isn't a bad time…"

"No, no. It's the perfect time now. New salt only coming in later today. A demon you say? Where?"

"Table Mountain. Near the Citadel."

"This have something to do with your job with the Titan Mages?"

"Was patrolling last night. Met a horned man who then broke my sword and sent me fleeing to sleep in a cave."

"Sounds like a fun evening. Can you describe this demon?"

"Looked human. Smart, black suit. Modern-looking. Sharp features and black hair. Only discernible non-human trait were the black horns."

"No wings?"

"Not that I saw."

"Could be hiding them or could materialise them at will..." Cindy contemplated, almost to herself.

"Any ideas?" I asked.

"There're a lot of demons out there, Kat. What I do know is that the ones that take human form tend to be the most dangerous. I'd be careful."

"He admitted to killing the Titan mages."

The words were out before I could stop myself. That was meant to be classified information. But this was Cindy. I could trust her. I think.

"Titan mages are dying?" she asked, doubtful, but with a hint of worry. I didn't reply. She continued. "If you insist, then I'd look through the UCT libraries. There are some good records on demons of the Cape. I'd study them in depth. See if you can find any stories. Demons love narratives. Stories are powerful."

I recalled the spectral horseman of Tokai manor, who I still doubted was the actual ghost of Frederick Eksteen, but rather an otherworldly spectre linked to the myth of the Earthly ghost story.

"Thanks, Cindy. I'll look into it."

"Cheers, Kat. Let me know if you need anything else. And I must stress this again – be careful. Demons aren't like the undead. They don't play by our rules, or even their own."

We hung up.

"Off to the archives, then?" Treth asked.

"You have a problem with that?" I whispered. I didn't want any other students thinking I was talking to myself.

"Not anymore. This demon is a threat. An evil threat. He, or it, needs to be stopped."

"Good. We're on the same page."

"Pfft…let's go do some studying."

I found myself going deeper and deeper into the depths of the UCT library. Down spiral staircases, down dusty steps and into the cold halls of the archives. Students called this part of library "the dungeon". They weren't that far off. It was cold, congested and grey. I could easily imagine its multitudes of rooms, halls and vaults housing decrepit prisoners. Yet, somehow it was my favourite place on campus. Beyond the rows of revising students and the shelves that received more attention, were an abundance of tomes dating back to the 19th century, let alone pre-Cataclysm. It was as if I was staring back in time, smelling the musty, pleasant scent of the ages. It was a place where dust became wonderful and the silence allowed one to contemplate the epochs. I didn't need to be a student of history to adore the dungeon. Anyone with any sort of sense would find themselves never wanting to leave this knowledge-filled, chilly hall.

"It's cold," Treth said, a slight shiver to his voice. "Isn't there any place in this subterranean prison with some form of warmth?"

"Didn't know ghosts could feel the cold," I whispered, walking quietly past some students studying on the first floor underneath the more popularly visited parts of UCT library.

"Ssshhh," a studier hushed me, despite my whispering. I hunched and beat a hasty retreat towards a swinging utility door, down into the dungeon proper.

"I'm not a ghost," Treth said, when we were alone in the stairwell.

"I could have sworn you said you were one."

Treth shrugged.

"The quest to discover the true nature of my roommate continues," I muttered. Treth snorted. Despite the awkwardness and acidic taste that my run in with Trudie and Andy had left, I found myself grinning at my spirit comrade.

An end to the stairs signalled the end of my journey. There was an immediate bite to the air. No sun or heaters to keep this area warm. Only air conditioning and dehumidifiers to ensure that the troves of UCT's literary treasures survived.

"How does one traverse such a vast hoard?" Treth asked, hushed. He had only been here once before, and he had been in one of his rare silences.

I quickly surveyed the room. I neither saw nor heard anyone that would think me mad.

"Digitally," I replied, whipping out Trudie's phone and going to the UCT library's website. Most of the library's collection was listed on their public registry. I typed the keywords "Cape" and "Demons" into the search bar.

After scrolling through some texts on sexual morality in the early Cape, I found a promising treatise – Cape Demons and Folklore.

"781.5 A. C," I muttered.

"Hmmm?"

"The catalogue number."

"What does it mean?"

"It is the location of the book. How do you not know this? We started university at the same time. We both went through library orientation."

"I wasn't paying attention."

"At least I'm being a dutiful student."

Treth snorted. He disagreed.

I stepped into the dungeon proper and scanned the exposed shelves. Many of the spines had no text. They were too old for spine-text. The types of books where you had to look at the first page to find the title. I seldom came to the dungeon. My majors kept me above ground, among the recent history and undead studies textbooks. I felt a regret that that was the case. The smell of old books and the pleasant quietness of this place was enchanting. I could be lost here, if only for a while, and genuinely enjoy it. Even find solace within it. Alas, these books were kept so low underground because they were less relevant to the modern-day student. Only the most niche graduate student could be found perusing their archival halls. A shame, really.

My meticulous studying of the library cataloguing system paid off, but the smell and beautiful hides of the countless tomes still delayed me from completing my task. Eventually, I twisted the vault-like handle on a row of shelves, creating a gap between two rows which my thin frame could invade.

I followed the book numbers, decimal by decimal. Mythology, folklore, fantasy that some thought non-fiction. All of it was pre-Cataclysm, but as my run-in with the spectral horseman of Tokai had taught me, pre-Cataclysm stories could be just as important as what came after the Vortex.

Finally, I found a red-bound tome with 781.5 A. C stuck on the spine. I retrieved it. The paper was fragile. That thin paper you often found in Bibles and psalm books. At least, the type of paper I remembered from church when my parents were still around to push me to go. I gave the book a sniff to take in the ancient scent and then started reading.

***

Jan van Hunks missed his days as a pirate. Not all of them, of course. He didn't miss the bouts of scurvy, the fright when a merchant ship was armed more than expected, or the brawls over loot, but he would have taken all that if he could have the freedom again. A pirate's life was filled with terror, hardship and wanton acts of extreme violence, but it was free. Free from the blasted woman that Jan called his wife, at least.

What was the problem if he wanted to smoke his pipe at home? It was his home! Paid for by him, with a little help from the Portuguese merchant fleet, of course. He had earned his retirement, fair and square. Bought himself and his wife a decent enough cottage at the foot of Table Mountain and had enough money to spare to live his life in frugal luxury till his arthritis, cannon-wrought tinnitus and perhaps an old privateer caught up with him.

Until then, all Jan wanted was to swig his rum and smoke his pipe. But that harpy of a woman wouldn't allow him even that simple pleasure. Said that the so-called putrid smoke clouded the house. No point in living in an area with such clean air if all he was going to do was pollute it with his acrid, albeit powerful, tobacco smog. And neither did she like his boisterousness after he partook of his rum – the pirate fuel. All in all, Jan was a second-class citizen in his own home.

Jan had been a pirate in his youth, however. And pirates always find a way.

So, every day, Jan scaled the steep slope up Table Mountain until his need for a puff overwhelmed his need to get away from his wife. Sometimes, he stopped on a low escarpment, a small jaunt away from the settlement. Other times, he went higher, sitting on the side of a rockface, his legs swinging over the abyss.

Today of all days, however, Jan went higher. He had received an earful from his wife that morning. He admittedly wasn't paying attention to what she had been saying but knew that he didn't want to be home for a while. He had stockpiled a decent amount of pipe tobacco, his own strong mix. It was more than enough for a few hours on the peak. If he smoked slowly, it could last him days, even.

So, Jan hiked and scrambled up to the flat-bed top of the mountain that dominated the Cape, until there was no sound but that of the wind and his heart beating from his exertion. He had to remind himself that he wasn't a young buccaneer anymore.

Jan had climbed to the peak often enough before. Often enough to have a favourite smoking place. A rock overlooking the bay. A large boulder was located behind said rock, providing pleasant shade and protection from the Cape winds. He caught his breath and made his way to his claimed rock. As he approached, however, he found that he was not alone. A stranger sat by his rock, on a rock of his own. As if waiting for Jan to take his seat. Of course, that was silly. This was a stranger, after all. They'd not know Jan's habits. This stranger was like Jan himself. A man pushed from sea-level, up and up into solitude.

Jan, unafraid, walked closer. The stranger, Jan now saw, was clothed in a black suit, with a black, wide-brimmed hat to match. He was sitting with his legs apart, watching the soil below his feet. So deep in thought that he didn't comment when Jan sat down on his rock opposite him.

Jan raised his eyebrow at the stranger, especially at his silence. When someone came within speaking distance, you spoke to them. Or at least acknowledged their presence with a glance and a nod. This black clothed man did neither. Was he asleep?

Jan drew out his pipe, a long wooden piece. An antique from his pirating days. He decanted his mix into the pipe and brought out a flint and steel to light it.

A click, click, and a spark brought the wonderful acrid scent into Jan's nostrils and mouth. He inhaled, and then exhaled. Bliss.

"Can I join you with that, good man?"

The sudden question from the stranger made Jan jump. The stranger looked at him, with a cordial close-mouthed smile. His features were young, unscarred by the ravages of time or hard work. His nose was sharp. His eyes were intense, but Jan found them comforting rather than unsettling. They were the eyes of a young man who had not learnt to cloud his vision with apathy and mistrust.

"I find myself with a pipe and tobacco, but without a light," the stranger continued.

Jan looked at his flint and steel, lying by him on his rock. He picked them up and passed them to the stranger, who lit his own pipe. Jan watched as the stranger's small smile turned into a wide grin of relief and joy. The stranger inhaled, and then exhaled a ring of smoke, that was promptly carried away by the wind.

"Thank you, good man. It is such a terrible thing to have the world at one's fingertips, but to have forgotten the key."

Jan grunted in agreement. He was a man of few words. The stranger returned the flint and steel and then carried on puffing contently. Jan continued to smoke in silence, looking out over the Cape. The stranger was also quiet.

They were silent for the entire meeting, until, finally, the stranger packed up his pipe and left. Jan nodded his goodbyes. The stranger smiled and disappeared in the distance. Jan returned home to a wife that complained that his clothing smelled like smoke.

The next day, Jan felt compelled to scale to the top of the mountain again. Like clockwork, the stranger was there to meet him once again. This time, the stranger had brought his own flint and steel, but had forgotten his pipe. Jan had extras, however, and shared. They smoked in relative silence, only passing comment at the rare ship that came to dock at the waterfront. Then, they departed like the day before.

Days followed, and Jan and the stranger met every day. It was odd, their relationship, but one that Jan came to cherish. Long silences, enjoying their tobacco and the occasional comment. It helped that the stranger had complimented Jan's tobacco mix. Jan prided himself on not much else.

One day, Jan arrived at the usual time to meet the stranger, who was already smoking. The stranger nodded in greeting and Jan nodded back.

There was the usual silence for just a bit, and then the stranger spoke.

"It is a clear day today. Not much wind. It makes me feel quite energetic."

Jan grunted in response, decanting tobacco into his pipe.

"How about," the stranger said, orientating himself to face the now seated Jan, "we have a bit of a contest?"

Jan raised his eyebrow.

"Only if there is a wager involved," Jan answered, his unlit pipe in his hand. While he did not like this energy, he was a man of solemn long silences after all, he was also a gambling man at heart. A pirate needed to be. "A contest is only worth anything if there's something at stake."

The stranger laughed. "Isn't that going a bit too fast? We haven't established the competition yet."

Jan held up his pipe. "We do what we usually do, but this time, with stakes. Nobody has ever outsmoked me. I doubt anyone on Earth could outsmoke Jan van Hunks."

Jan was a man of few words, but not a humble man.

"Excellent idea! And the wager?"

Jan shrugged. He didn't know what to wager. He had everything he wanted.

"How about: your soul against the kingdoms of the world?"

Perplexed, Jan raised his eyebrow. The stranger grinned, showing his teeth and then roared in laughter.

"Not that ambitious? Well, then. Your soul against a bottle of red gold rum."

Jan grinned. He loved his rum. And who needed a soul anyway? He offered his hand to agree to the terms. The stranger accepted, and they shook. Despite Jan's superior muscles and more callused hands, the stranger had an impressive grip.

"I find myself without any more tobacco, however. Would you share your mix with me? It smells...impressive."

Jan nodded. He enjoyed showing off his mix. The stranger deposited some leaves into his pipe and lit it. Jan did the same.

They began.

It started out like every other time. They smoked in silence. Smoked and smoked. But this time, neither of them stopped. The stranger did not stand to leave, and Jan did not go home to his wife. They smoked and smoked. When their pipes ran out, they replaced the tobacco with more. Yet, the more leaves they took from Jan's stash, the more the stash seemed to grow in size. Jan knew that after the sun set, darkness fell, and then the sun rose again, that he should be tired, hungry and parched. But he was not. All that mattered was the pipe in his mouth and the stranger smoking in front of him.

Days passed, and the sky filled with their smoke. It spread out so heavily that not even the Cape's legendary gusts of wind could push them away. Rather, the smog settled on top of Table Mountain, forming an appropriate tablecloth. Days turned to weeks. Months. The tobacco never ran out, and Jan's humanness was forgotten. So was his wife, that he had loved once. All that mattered was the pipe in his hand and the smoke billowing from it.

Finally, when the haze of the smoke formed a very real cloud over the entirety of Table Mountain's peak, one that would return for all time, the stranger facing Jan coughed. Kept smoking. Then coughed again. His cough turned into a sputter, and he promptly doubled over, retching.

Jan noted two things. First, was the complete elation that he had won. Second, the stranger's wide-brimmed hat had fallen off, revealing a pair of horns.

Jan's pipe fell from his lips and he uttered, despite the dryness of his throat. "The devil himself!"

"Yes, and I do not like losing a wager."

There was no hint of the cordiality that had once defined Jan's strange companion. No civil grin or good humour, but a snarl that twisted the youthful face into a demonic visage.

"I beat you fair and square, devil!" Jan shouted, over the howling wind that now threatened to deafen him. Wreathes of smoke and flame replaced the stranger's black clothes. A pair of bat-like wings erupted from his back.

"And I will not take your soul. You will get your precious rum, Van Hunks, but you shall not be able to return home to drink it. You shall stay here, for all time. You shall form this tablecloth of smoke for future generations. An eternity to regret besting me."

Jan did not reply. He could not. With those words, his humanity was struck from him. The devil dispersed, as if he was never there, but Jan remained, involuntarily smoking his pipe. Forever, and ever.

***

So, that's what caused the tablecloth, Table Mountain's iconic cloud cover. Well, assuming the story was true. And that was an unsafe assumption. Modern science had plenty of explanations for clouds. But the story was interesting nonetheless. It revealed that there was a demonic myth in the Cape and, if my forays into demonology had taught me anything, demon stories should not be scoffed at. There was power to a story, even if it was just a story. Van Hunks, as real or fictitious as he may be, believed the stranger to be the devil. The problem with that assessment was that post-Cataclysmic denizens now understood that there was not one devil. There were many. In fact, it was one of the most populous sub-categories of demons.

Horned, wily creatures, often with bat-like wings and cloven hooves. While all demons were threatening, devils weren't considered all that special. The creature in this book didn't sound like a devil. Rather, it sounded like one of the arch-demons of Judeo-Christian tradition. The unenlightened interchangeably referred to every demon as the devil, however, making discerning the identity of such a demon difficult.

"If only we could find a name," I muttered, paging through the rest of the book to no avail. It was a collection of folk stories, not a treatise on an obscure demon of Cape mythology.

"There can't be too many demon names to go through," Treth offered.

"Doesn't matter. If I had a name, I could banish it with a little help from our neighbourhood purifier. But if I use the wrong name, the demon could use that vulnerability to curse or even destroy me outright."

"Not worth the risk…"

"You don't think?" I answered sarcastically. I returned the book to its shelf and rubbed my temples. The story was interesting, but it didn't bring me any closer to figuring out how to defeat the demon. But what had Cindy said?

"Stories are powerful. Demons like narratives," I muttered to myself. I felt Treth nod. He also remembered it.

"There must be something in the story. That rock where we met the demon sounds too eerily similar for it to just be a coincidence."

I nodded. "He also mentioned some stuff...I cannot recall outright. Was a bit distracted."

"He mentioned a smoking competition and cursing someone," Treth said. "I am pretty sure these demons are one and the same."

"Still doesn't bring us any closer to defeating him..."

"Kat?" a voice sounded. To my credit, I didn't jump, but I did reach for my swords that weren't there. I was lucky too, that they weren't there, as the source of the voice was Colin Philips, my one-time pro-bono attorney. He'd helped me get off a murder case. Well, a vigilantism case. He was peering between the gaps of the bookshelves, carrying a stack of books underneath his one arm.

"Colin? What are you doing here?" I tried to hide my fluster at the surprise but failed.

He indicated the book pile. "Alumni can still use the library. Was picking up some legal history books."

"For work?"

"For fun."

It takes all types.

I sidled out of the narrow movable bookshelf aisle and was re-acquainted with the chill of the dungeon.

"So, Kat...how've things been?"

I shrugged. "Same old. You?"

"Work's been going well. How did your date go?"

My cheeks involuntarily reddened.

"Date? What date?" I asked fast.

"Your goth friend was speaking loud enough for the entire mall to hear. Lecturing you on everything from fashion to cinema etiquette."

Trudie. Damn Trudie. Couldn't she be a bit quieter? Well, that was in the past. Trudie wasn't telling me how to date Andy now. She was dating Andy. I couldn't really articulate how that made me feel.

"Date didn't...go as planned. Ran into a monster."

"Sounds like your usual night."

I snorted in amusement. "Yeah, quite."

"And?"

"This an interrogation?"

Colin grinned, almost boyishly. I noted that his smile was kinda cute. His glasses suited him. Made him look nerdy, but the same way Clark Kent looked nerdy. There was nothing wrong with being nerdy. I'd like to call myself a nerd, but my active workout regime prevented me from that privilege. Unless we're judging nerdiness by obsession with niche topics. Then I'm definitely a nerd. My niche is just a bit more violent than most.

"Habit," he said. "Been cross examining and interviewing witnesses and clients for weeks now."

"Let's just say that the guy and I didn't see eye to eye."

"A lot of rhyming there."

I couldn't help but grin. That was nerdy, but the rhyming was half on purpose. I appreciated that he noticed.

An awkward silence followed as I didn't reply. I saw Colin fidget a bit with his book.

"Well...uh...don't want to keep you any longer. You must be busy."

"Ah, yeah."

Colin began walking off.

"Colin..."

He stopped and turned.

"Um…nice running into you here. Would you…uh…possibly like to hang out sometime?"

Colin smiled. "That'd be great."

I gave him my number and he gave his to me as my cheeks flushed red. After he left, I found myself standing in the middle of the now empty dungeon.

"So…" Treth said. "Kat likes a boy?"

"Shut up, Treth," I said, but couldn't help but smile.

Chapter 10.Necro

"Didn't see you come in last night," Mrs Ndlovu said as I greeted her outside my apartment building. She was wiping the grit off an 'Enter at your own risk' sign. It was a new addition. She suspected a gremlin might have taken residence in the building after a few inhabitants had to replace some broken lightbulbs. "Or leave this morning."

"Went camping," I said with a genuine smile. I liked my landlady. She was very forgiving when I couldn't pay my rent on time. Her eccentricities were a small price to pay, if they were even a price.

I made my way to my apartment where a very angry Alex greeted me.

"I'm sorry, boy," I told him in a baby voice, squatting to stroke him. He refused my advances and ran to his food bowl.

I didn't like my cat being angry at me. Someone needed to pay for causing such a thing.

My phone rang and the caller immediately gave me someone on which to vent my anger.

"Kat," Conrad said, I didn't let him finish.

"The entire night, Conrad. You know where I was for the entirety of last night?"

"The peak?"

"The fucking peak."

"Sorry about that," he said, sounding genuinely bashful. "I've already spoken to Charlotte, the liaison. She says she'll make sure the guards are disciplined."

I didn't respond. I hoped my ire could be felt through the phone. I moved to Alex and opened a sachet of cat food with one hand. It was some gourmet cat food. More expensive than the stuff I was eating. I really needed to look after myself more…

"Well," Conrad said. "Did you find anything?"

"A demon," I said, still a hint of anger in my voice, but it was abating. "Already spoken to Cindy Giles about it and looked it up. Connected to some old Cape myth."

"And?"

"It admitted to killing the mages."

A pause.

"What did Cindy say?"

"To be careful and to pay attention to narratives."

"Do that then. Cindy knows her stuff."

"I will."

I was about to hang up when he spoke again.

"Kat, I got some info on the Necrolord."

That got my attention.

"What is it?"

"General quietness in the slums. Too quiet, actually. A lot of the gang wars have stopped. It is as if something has united them. A *Leviathan*, of some sorts."

"Hobbes?"

"Yeah, unless a giant sea monster is dominating the slum gangs. Anyway, the slums have been too quiet. That was until an entire block disappeared. Not the buildings, of course, but all the people. At least a hundred, just vanished."

I frowned. Trudie had vanished alongside all the guests at the *Eternity Lounge*. The necromancer had admitted to abducting her for the Blood Cartel.

"Sounds like my necromancer's MO."

"Yeah. Thought you'd like to know."

"Thanks, Conrad. So, when do I get on the case?"

"Not now, Kat. You've got a high paying contract with the Citadel. Focus on that demon. Don't be distracted."

"But…"

"No buts. The Necrolord will see justice eventually. You don't need to go swimming in the slums when you should be on top of Table Mountain."

Begrudgingly, I nodded even though he couldn't see me. My silence was assent enough for him though.

"Good. Keep me updated on the hunt."

"I will."

He hung up.

"Let's get rid of this demon so we can focus on the primary villain," Treth said.

"That assumes we can get rid of the demon."

"What demon?" Duer asked, floating down from his bird-house abode.

"A smartly dressed bastard on top of the mountain."

"Why'd someone dress smartly to go up a mountain?" Duer asked.

"Pride, probably," I responded. "He seemed pretty prideful."

"He did," Treth added, even though Duer could not hear him. "Prideful enough to start a contest and then screw with the wager when he lost."

"Pride is a cardinal sin," I said.

"By whose measure?"

"No one that matters, but there is a reason that pride is considered a vice."

"And what is that?"

"Pride cometh before the fall."

"Says you."

"Hahaha," I said sarcastically. "But it is something to think about."

"You think you can twist his hubris to your advantage?" Treth sounded doubtful.

"Demons aren't perfect beings. Very far from it. Power always has its weaknesses. This demon seems to love a challenge and gets testy when he fails at it."

"Only time we knew he beat someone, that someone was cursed to make clouds for eternity," Treth reminded me.

"Sure, but…that demon seemed kinda wistful about it. As if he regretted it."

"Wouldn't trust a demon on looks alone."

"Yeah, yeah. But…it does suggest something we can use."

Treth silently awaited my plan. Duer was bored of my seeming insanity and went to do whatever pixies do when they're squatting in a human's apartment.

"Demons love narratives. That demon seemed sad that he had no one to smoke with. No one to re-enact the old story. If someone challenges him to a new wager, he will probably accept."

"To what ends? Even if you win, he will just curse you like he did Van Hunks."

"He didn't betray the wager, however. Van Hunks got his rum and didn't lose his soul. He was just enslaved."

"*Just* enslaved."

"Van Hunks was going in blind. He thought the wager was a joke. If I phrase the wager properly, I could avoid such a curse."

"Maybe... But still too risky. And even if you can figure out a good wager, how are you going to beat him? He may only accept a challenge like last time. You don't smoke."

"I don't," I agreed. "But I know someone who does."

Chapter 11. The Tablecloth

"At least eat before you go ahead with whatever you're planning," Treth pleaded.

"Yes, mom..." I fake whined and put some toast on. I got some peanut butter out of the breadbin. A new breadbin, I might add, paid for by the Titan Citadel's patrol fee. No more stale bread for me.

"Who are you going to get to help?" Treth asked, as I waited for my toast to pop.

"A seasoned smoker."

I felt Treth about to press, but then felt his realisation of my plan.

"You can't! She'd never go for it."

"She will if I ask."

"She's a civilian, Kat. And your friend."

My toast popped, and I began buttering it.

"Nothing will happen to her."

"This is a demon we're talking about."

"Demons play by their own rules, but they do have rules. This demon follows the rules of the competition. He did not betray Van Hunks' wager, for instance, nor did he cheat at the contest. I must only be careful to phrase the wager properly and ensure I can win it."

"And how are you going to do that?"

"You remember what the demon said when we found him that night?"

"His discussion about missing Van Hunks?"

"While that is interesting, no. He mentioned that he had not smoked in a long time. While I'm no expert on a demon's skill retention, if the demon failed to beat a mortal then, it should fail to beat a mortal now."

"But what if you're wrong? What if Trudie isn't as skilled a smoker as you'd believed?"

What if I'm wrong? Will I let Trudie suffer for my hubris? No...

"I'll ensure that she won't be harmed."

Treth was doubtful.

I took a bite of my toast just as I heard a knock at the door. Who could that be?

I peered through the eye-hole, munching on peanut butter and toast. As if by prophecy, Trudie was on the other side, and (mercifully) Andy-less.

I opened the door.

"Hey, Kat," Trudie smiled, but I detected a hint of awkwardness in her expression and gait. She was wearing a white and black striped skirt with a crimson pseudo-leather jacket. Her hands were in her jacket pockets and she was rocking on the balls of her feet. "I heard you talking. Someone here?"

"Hey. No, no. No one here. Phone fixed already?"

Trudie passed me my phone. "Was odd. One minute, it was if the entire thing had fried and then the next it was powering up fine."

That was odd. I smiled, faintly. "Well, all credit to the techie."

"Yeah…"

I exchanged my SIM card out of my borrowed phone and put it into my phone.

"Anyway, I'll be off…" Trudie began to turn around.

"Wait…"

She stopped. I froze.

I'd been so cocksure before. The plan was concrete. After dissecting the story, I felt I knew this demon. Understood this demon enough to defeat him. I was so confident in my plan that I even thought I could bring my best friend into it. What had happened last time my friend went along with me into my world?

Pranish. He helped me save Trudie. And what had happened to him? Could I risk such a thing happening to

Trudie? Could I risk my bubbly, nagging, ever-reliable and caring friend?

And did I have a choice?

"This about Andy?"

My breath caught in my throat. Oh, Rifts, I couldn't talk about that...

"No!" I said, a little too fast and a little too loudly.

Trudie faced me and put her hands on her hips.

"What's going on, Kat?"

Was I going to do this? Trudie's glare dug into my soul. Not only did I need her help now, I needed to mend this brewing conflict between us. She was my friend, and while we hadn't been spending a lot of time together recently, and while this thing with Andy threatened to put a huge divide between us, I still wanted to be her friend.

"Trudie, I need your help," I finally said, with a resigned sigh.

She cocked her head. My tone and the question itself shifted her expression from one of anticipatory defensiveness to one of concern. That was the look I preferred on Trudie's face. That, and her sleeping. She was very cute when she was asleep.

"My help?" Trudie asked, contemplating what that help might involve. "Only computer-anything you have is your phone, which I just fixed. That means you don't need me to fix anything. Need help shopping?"

"No, Trudie. I've got this job…"

Trudie raised her eyebrow. "You need my help on a job?"

I nodded.

"Slaying monsters?"

I shook my head. "Not exactly."

I noticed now that she was still standing outside, her back to the outdoors where we could smell car fumes and hear the noises of Rondebosch. I moved to the side and indicated for my friend to enter. She looked dubious, but then went inside. Alex purred at her approach and she bent down to stroke him.

"What's going on, Kat?" Trudie asked, after I closed the door. Alex was purring like a machine-gun. He had flopped onto his back and accepted Trudie's belly rubs graciously.

"I've been working a case for the Titan Citadel," I said.

"For the Cult? That's some heavy-hitter stuff, Kat. But why do you need me?"

"The monster I'm meant to eliminate isn't my usual fare…"

"Hmmm?"

I sighed. "I can't kill it. But I think I've figured out a way to get rid of it without killing it?"

Alex looked perturbed as Trudie stood and looked at me.

Last chance to back out.

"I need someone who can out-smoke a demon."

Too late.

"Out-smoke a demon?" Trudie's unnaturally black eyebrow looked about to disappear beyond her fringe.

"It sounds silly, but demons often are."

"Aren't demons dangerous?"

"Definitely, but they have rules. They like to play games. This one is linked to an old Cape myth. He challenged an old pirate to a smoking contest and lost."

"So, what makes you think this demon will accept a challenge from me? And if he does, what makes you think I can beat him?"

"Because he's proud and because he's out of practice. You are well-practiced."

She creased her forehead, in thought. A big part of me hoped she refused. If she did, I could find another way. Perhaps, a way that didn't risk my best friend.

"Do you think your plan will work?" Trudie asked.

I hesitated, but then nodded.

"Well," she sighed. "You haven't failed before. I'm in. But I may have a better idea…"

I didn't know if I should be relieved or terrified.

***

Whiteshield was walking on egg-shells around me after I kicked up a storm due to their leaving me on the mountain all night. Lucky for me, as they caused minimal fuss in allowing Trudie to accompany me to the top. My friend's initial trepidation at the guards and going up a forbidden mountain at night was replaced with ecstatic delight at the cable car and the sight of Hope City's night lights. The shimmering yellows, reds and oranges of our city's lights in the darkness were enchanting.

We reached the top at around 8pm. There was still a little bit of red in the sky as the sun refused to give up its attention on Hope City. We had a packed dinner and we sat down at a table I presumed would usually be used by guards during their lunch break. The dinner was Chinese.

Trudie ordered sweet and sour chicken with rice and I ordered spicy crispy pork with noodles. Yum!

After we were finished, there was a silence. A long, awkward silence that had seemed to be becoming common between us.

Trudie stared into the distance, towards the star-like field of skyscraper lights of Old Town just behind us. It truly was a wonderful view. It was like looking over the world itself. Or into space. Did the realms beyond the Vortex look like this from afar? Did Treth's world look like a mere speck from where we sat? I looked up towards the real stars. They were clearer up here. Crisper. Could one of those stars be the sun of Treth's world? Would we ever know?

"Ground Control to Major Tom," David Bowie sang from Trudie's vibrating cell, located on the bench next to a soy sauce stained polystyrene container. She picked up and answered.

"Hey, Andy. Yeah. With Kat. Hmmm? Yeah. A job."

She looked at me. I tried my best to look impassive.

"Not sure. Will see you tomorrow. Yeah. Bye, baby."

Baby? Oh, Rifts. I'm gonna be sick!

"That was Andy," she said, as if I didn't know already. "Wanted to hang out."

She noticed my expression. I realised I was frowning.

"What's with that look?"

"What look?" When in doubt – deny everything.

"That look." Trudie scowled. "You looked like you wanted to throw my cell off the cliff."

Must have been more a growl than a frown then…

Before I could respond, Trudie looked away, and sighed. Heavily.

"Why, Kat?"

"Why what?"

"Is it because you're jealous? I'm sorry that I'm dating your ex. Okay? But, I really like him. And you just shut him out so quickly…"

"He's not my ex…" I muttered. And that was the truth. Went on one failed date and one fake date. Then I realised that he was a… I don't even know what.

"Shady as a Shadowtown peddler," Treth offered.

"But you're still jealous?" Trudie raised an accusatory eyebrow while she lit a cigarette.

"You sure you want to start now? You could be smoking for hours with this guy if the plan doesn't work."

"Warming up and answer the question."

I looked out into the black, towards the Citadel, barely even a silhouette now in the dark. I felt Trudie's gaze pierce my flesh. I gave my own sigh.

"I'm not jealous. At least, I don't think I am."

"Then what's up?" Her voice wasn't angry. It was sincere. She really wanted to know what I was feeling. Not for her own sake, but because we were friends and she cared about me.

"I don't trust him."

"Because he didn't risk his life on some fool's errand against a vampire cartel. He isn't you, Kat."

"You were the fool's errand, Trudie."

"Well, thanks."

I looked at her, a bit irritated that she used such a sarcastic tone when Pranish and I'd risked our lives for her, but then I saw tears in her eyes. She took a drag and continued.

"Andy isn't like you, Kat. But he doesn't need to be. I've got you already."

She took another long drag, blew out a cloud of smoke right into my face, and said. "Only need one of you."

I could not help but smile. Faintly, but Trudie noticed. I suspected that, at least for a little while, we'd be okay.

"What's that?" Trudie asked, looking over my shoulder. I turned and saw a little spark of light in the distance. It was coming from where it had last night. The demon had arrived.

"Our demon," I said. Trudie must have noticed the professional coldness in my tone. I saw her become apprehensive. She didn't stand as I did.

I had to remember, this wasn't like my usual cases. I had my best friend with me. Needed to be a friend.

I smiled a reassuring smile and offered my hand to my friend. In the gesture, I hoped I conveyed a simple but powerful message:

"I'll protect you."

Trudie looked at my hand, took it and stood up. I led her into the darkness.

"Are we really doing this?"

"Hunting a demon? Yeah..."

"No, walking in pitch black on top of a mountain."

"Oh, sorry." I turned on my flashlight. It still wasn't ideal. Trudie almost tripped a lot. She was wearing boots instead of heels, but she wasn't as dextrous or as balanced as I. The fynbos and brambles were catching her. Hopefully, we wouldn't need to run. I frowned in the darkness. If we had to run, I had the terrible feeling we wouldn't be fast enough.

My flashlight's pool of illumination hit the side of the boulder from the Van Hunks story and, as was to be expected, the demon was sitting at his usual place, twiddling a lit pipe in his hands. He looked the same as he had the other night. A black suit. Tall. Sullen.

"He really a demon?" Trudie whispered.

I gulped and nodded.

"He's kinda hot."

I rolled my eyes.

"Back again, Ms Drummond?" the demon asked. He sounded too human to be an otherworldly monster. If Cindy was to be believed, the most human monsters were the most dangerous.

"My friend and I would like to challenge you…"

"Call me Jan."

"Jan was the man you cursed. What is your real name?"

Unexpectedly, the demon laughed. A full, loud laugh, with his face to the sky.

"You really ask a demon his real name, Ms Drummond?"

"Wouldn't it be fair? You know my name."

"Life, like games, isn't fair, Kat Drummond and Trudie Davidson. Call me Jan or call me demon. Your choice."

Trudie's grip on my hand tightened at the comment. I didn't blame her. Didn't like strangers knowing my name. At least it wasn't our true name. Well, it could be Trudie's true name. We didn't know each other's true names. Safer that way. If anyone got hold of our true names, this demon included, we could have all manner of curses and destruction magic sent at us from afar.

"Okay, demon. I come to challenge you, as Van Hunks challenged you centuries before, but this time with the knowledge of what you are capable of."

"Intriguing," the demon responded, unimpressed by my self-assured tone. "What type of contest? Don't tell me a duel. You saw what I did last night. It wouldn't be fair."

He put emphasis on the last word, mockingly. He was right though. Wouldn't be fair. In a fight, I'd die. Question was: would Trudie and I die if my other plan didn't work?

"You had a contest here with Jan van Hunks around three centuries ago. You smoked and smoked, until he beat you. Then, you tricked him and cursed him to form the tablecloth. We seek to challenge you to such a contest again, but with no tricks. We come into this with the knowledge of your demonic nature and can thus make a proper wager."

"Thus? Are you writing an essay?" The light from my flashlight caught on the demon's smirk. "What are your terms?"

Was he really going for it? Phew! Next step…

"Before the wager – the rules. Games might not be fair, but they have rules."

The demon nodded, almost unconsciously. He agreed. I hoped it wasn't a subtle trick.

"My friend and you will smoke the same brand of cigarettes. You shall not use magic or demonic trickery to stretch the supply of cigarettes or enchant the flow of time. The winner will be decided by whomever can finish three packs of cigarettes before the other. If neither of you is finished by sunrise, the one with the least cigarettes left will win."

"A race then? A neat twist. It works. I don't have all night, after all. Much less the months that I spent with Van

Hunks," the demon said. "And the wager? You won't accept the *kingdoms of the world?*"

"If my friend, Trudie, wins, you shall stop killing the Titan mages. You will leave this mortal plane instantly. Additionally, you shall not harm nor curse any of us. You shall leave us be with our victory."

The demon nodded. "And if I win?"

"If we lose: you can have my soul."

Trudie's hand tightened on mine. I felt her gaze on me.

"Your soul?" The demon's grin cut his face in two like the Cheshire Cat from Alice in Wonderland. He didn't look that human anymore. "Why would I want such a battered and broken thing? Even if there are two of them, they are not worth anything to me. What else can you wager?"

Battered and broken? It also seemed the demon detected Treth. Well, would deal with that later.

"If you win…" I began again. "I will serve you on Earth."

"What?" Treth asked, aghast. He didn't expect that. Neither did I. But what else was I supposed to offer? I thought demons loved souls but apparently mine is too cheap even for them.

"Are you sure, Kat?" Trudie whispered, almost a whimper. She wasn't as confident in her plan now. I looked at her in the dark. She looked like a vampire in this light. I smiled, weakly.

"Serve me? Interesting..."

The demon rubbed his chin.

"I accept the wager."

I stopped myself from sighing in relief. The tricky part was done.

I walked towards the demon. Trudie, reluctantly, followed. I took my backpack off and took out six boxes of cigarettes. Trudie's brand. Don't ask me what made them special. She insisted they were the most hardcore brand, though. Only real punks like her smoked them (apparently).

I divided the pile into three for the demon and three for Trudie. Trudie took a seat on Van Hunks' rock and I stood in the centre, over the middle rock. The demon leaned over casually and picked up all three of his boxes. I noted that he smelled like Old Spice and fynbos. I offered him a gas station lighter. He declined. A flame emitted from his finger.

"I hid my nature from Van Hunks. No need to do so with you."

He leaned back and looked at my friend. She hadn't picked up the cigarette boxes yet. She clasped her lighter in her hand. Under her white makeup, I knew she was white as a sheet. Poor Trudie! I'd need to buy her something to make up for this. That is, if what we did worked.

"Are you going to start?" the demon asked, already smoking his cigarette.

I took a deep breath. Trudie leaned forward.

"Now!"

Gasoline poured from the now open front pocket of my bag. In a flash, Trudie lit her disposable lighter and tossed it onto the three cigarette boxes in the centre. The cigarettes were immolated instantly, not even leaving the stubs. As was the case with such powerful flames, it died quickly, leaving the smoking, stinking carcasses of charred tobacco, cardboard and plastic sleeves.

We both looked at the demon, his first cigarette hanging loosely from his lips. He looked as shocked as I'd ever think an otherworldly immortal could look.

"Trudie finished first," I said.

Silence.

Was he offended? Did he consider this cheating? Would he not accept the win?

"We won. Disappear."

But he didn't disappear. Instead, he frowned. A deeply mournful frown. He looked...ashamed.

"Congratulations, girls. You win."

"Good. Then go."

"I'm sorry, but I can't do that."

I instinctively moved to the side, putting myself in front of Trudie. She backed away as far as she could on her rock.

"The wager would have stood..." he said, a hint of disgust in his voice. "If I was my own demon. But, alas, my dear girls, another holds my reins."

In an instant, I saw purple-black tendrils reach out towards us. I felt their intense evil. They meant to curse, if not outright destroy me. And, after I was dead, Trudie would be next. I could not let that happen. But how could I stop it?

I was no purification mage. I wasn't some demon hunter. I was a student playing part-time monster hunter. This was way above my pay-grade, and my friend was going to suffer for it. But I stood my ground. I held my breath, and I didn't close my eyes.

The tendrils stopped a centimetre from my face, then dispersed. The demon looked just as shocked as I. He looked at his hands, and then at me. His smirk returned to his face, and he laughed.

"Interesting, Ms Drummond. Very interesting."

He disappeared.

All went quiet. My flashlight went off. I had the feeling Trudie would need to fix our phones again or wait for them to start working.

"That was amazing!"

Trudie's shout shook me out of my reverie.

"How did you do that? I didn't know you were a wizard. Did Pranish teach you?"

"What are you talking about?" I asked, genuinely.

"What do you mean? One second, he was pointing menacingly at us, and then you started glowing while chanting some spell. Then he disappeared like he was supposed to. I didn't take Pranish seriously before, but now I know. You really are cool! I want to come on another hunt. Do you ever hunt unicorns? Horse wannabe bastards."

I almost lost my balance as she hugged me tight.

I didn't smile. And I didn't feel relieved. I didn't know what had happened, but what I did know was that I hadn't seen the last of the demon.

Chapter 12. Dating

I had a gut feeling that this wasn't over, and if I had learned anything in this line of work, it was to trust my gut.

"The demon is gone, Kat! Let's get paid," Conrad pleaded.

"Not gone. He didn't fulfil the wager. Just disappeared."

"No murders for a week. Citadel is ready to pay us out."

"He's biding his time," I said, distracted by a stir fry I was cooking, my one hand on the wok-handle and my other on my cell phone. I was eating well of late. A lot of money to burn. I didn't even feel bad about spending it.

"You're overthinking," Conrad whined. What was he spending his money on anyway? His living expenses seemed pretty cheap.

"Give it another week. If the Citadel still wants to pay us then, then go right ahead."

"I didn't think I'd need to argue with someone about *them* getting paid," Conrad sighed. "Fine. A week."

He hung up.

It was mid-semester holidays and I was cooking myself a stir fry for lunch. Had a head of cabbage, bell pepper, onion, some cut up chicken and a lot of chilli. Would top it off with rice.

"Never thought you'd be one to turn down money," Treth said.

"If money was my prime motivator, I wouldn't be a hunter. I'd become a plumber or deep-sea welder."

"And have to contend with ratmen and merfolk? Those jobs are more dangerous than hunting!"

"But get paid a lot more on average. So, no. I don't just do this for the money, as hard as that may be for you to believe. That demon is still out there. He said so himself. I didn't finish my job. Can't in good conscience get paid."

"Very virtuous, miss knight. But while you're chasing a poofed demon, there are undead crawling out of their holes."

I frowned while tossing my stir fry. Treth was right. My primary enemy was still out there, while I hunted otherworldly immortals.

"Something's just not right. That demon isn't like anything we've hunted before," I pondered aloud.

"And that's why I'd rather take the money and get back to what we're used to fighting. Undead are safer."

"Heh. We're an odd bunch, aren't we?"

"I don't know about me," Duer interjected, flying down to investigate the stir fry. "But I know you're pretty odd. You putting honey on that?"

"You think I should?" I raised my eyebrow. I seldom cooked stir fry. When I did, I rarely experimented.

"I'd do it." Duer shrugged.

Well, couldn't hurt. It's just lunch. Duer brought me the honey squeeze bottle and I lathered the top layer of stir fry with honey, stirring it in and continuing to toss the pile. A savoury and sweet aroma rose from the conglomeration of meats and veggies, making my mouth water. I used my seax to skewer a piece of chicken and checked it for pinkness.

"I think it's done!"

I dished up into my single, overused food bowl and mixed it with my already cooked rice. Duer stared longingly enough at a piece of honey lathered red bell pepper that I poked it with my fork and put it on his saucer. He licked his lips and dug in.

"I thought you were vegetarian," I asked, between mouthfuls.

"Yeah. This is a vegetable."

"Mixed with meat."

Duer shrugged. "We aren't allergic to meat."

"Thought it was an ethical thing. Being a part of all nature and stuff like that."

I took another mouthful. Needed more chillies.

"Nothing like that," Duer took another bite. The piece was the size of his torso and he'd already eaten a portion as big as his head. He seemed to be enjoying it. "We just didn't get meat a lot. Try never eating something ever, and then eating it. It's gross. And less chilli next time."

"Heresy! More chilli."

Duer rolled his eyes. This was a fundamental dispute in values. There'd be no compromise.

My phone rang, playing some dark-wave goth stuff with heavy bass that Trudie put on when I wasn't looking. Duer jumped off his saucer and shot my cell a glare before returning to the bell pepper slice.

I wondered how much his petite frame could healthily put away before picking up the cell. The caller ID said "Colin".

I immediately flushed. Colin. What was he doing calling me? Well, I gave him my number. Of course, he was going to phone me. That's how it worked. Why did I give him my number though? I didn't usually give out my number.

Or did I? A lot of clients had my number. But Colin wouldn't be calling about a job. Or would he?

Oh, rifts. I'm rambling to myself!

The phone kept ringing.

Why did I give my number to Colin? Was it because…I liked him?

It rang again. I had to make a choice.

"Answer it!" Treth ordered. I pressed the receiver.

"Hey," both Colin and I said at the same time.

I paused. He paused.

"Howzit?" we both said, thinking the other was waiting for us.

By the Cataclysm and all the stranded gods, not this awkwardness. Well, at least it wasn't the silence I had with Andy.

"Pause, give him the initiative," Treth suggested.

I took the advice. There was a long pause. But before it grew too awkward, Colin spoke.

"Hey, Kat. Howzit?"

I almost sighed in relief. I really thought the pause would last longer. "I'm good, Colin. What you been up to?"

"Not much. Cases kinda dry at the moment. Just been doing office work."

"Sorry to hear that."

"Nah, it's cool. Gives me some time off. It's mid-semester holidays, right?"

I often forgot that Colin wasn't a student like me. He was a few years my senior and had a law degree. But as was often the case with genuine lawyers and not the types who just became lawyers because they watched some overhyped TV show, Colin kept tabs on the academics of his discipline.

"Yeah, it is."

"Hunts?"

"None at the moment."

"Cool. I was, uh, wondering if you'd like to go out for coffee. You know? For a change of pace."

My face reddened. Go out for coffee? Like a date? I did not have a good track record with dating.

"I'd love that!" I said unconsciously, and a little bit too eagerly. My inner voice scolded me. *Why you being so easy, Kat?* My inner voice then asked: *Does this mean you like him?*

"Great. You busy today?"

I paused, faking consideration. Even if it was my instincts making me act, I at least needed to be a bit charismatic. Couldn't be too easy. When I couldn't hold it much longer. "Nah. Let's meet. Café Henna? It's near my apartment."

"Sounds great. I can see you there in 45 minutes."

"Perfect!"

We said goodbye.

Silence. Duer stared up at me. Treth stared at me from his invisible ethereal chamber. Even Alex was considering me rather than my stir-fry.

"Kat likes a boy…" Treth and Duer both chimed.

Did I? My inability to argue with them suggested that that may very well be the case.

***

I wore my denim jeans (with the least blood stains) and my black leather jacket (with only three noticeable ghoul claw marks on the back), with a Fleetwood Mac t-shirt underneath. My dark chestnut hair was loose, coming down just past my shoulders. Duer had mocked me while giving me bad advice the entire time. Treth was surprisingly encouraging. Advised which clothing I should wear and even suggested I wear my hair loose for once.

Was very out of character for him. Last time I'd gotten close to any guy, Brett, Treth started whining like a steam train. Or at least what steam trains whined like in movies. No trains in Hope City anymore.

What made this time different? I didn't have long to think about it. I had a date. Or was it a date? I didn't really know. Did I want it to be a date? I didn't know that either.

I walked to Café Henna. It was located on Rondebosch main road, between a fast-food outlet that made students fat and the Chinese place that was the source of Trudie and my favourite takeaways. I was early. Of course, I was! Was it because I didn't spend enough time making myself look good? I didn't know how to do that. If only I had Trudie here to help.

Treth must have sensed my angst. "You're early because you live a few minutes away. Relax. You look great."

I couldn't help but blush. Treth seldom complimented me.

I sat down at a table for two, shifting my hidden knife in my jacket so it wouldn't poke into my ribs. This may be a friendly occasion, but I didn't go anywhere without at least one weapon. The attack at UCT and my lack of weapons at the time continued to scar me just a bit to this day. I also had two sachets of demanzite. Didn't know when you'd run into some uppity sorcerers.

I sent the waitress away twice to wait for my date (ignoring her pitying gaze) before Colin finally arrived.

"Sorry to keep you waiting!" he said, repressing some panting. I could see a sheen of sweat on his brow and he was red from minor exertion.

"No, my fault," I said earnestly, resisting a blush that I didn't understand. I tried to stand but knocked my knees into the table in front of me. He motioned that I didn't need to stand up. I smiled, relieved. He was wearing a business suit, tie and all. He put his jacket on the back of his chair and then took a seat.

"Work?" I asked.

"Always, but I wear this most of the time. Habit, and I kinda like it. Half the reason I wanted to be a lawyer. An excuse to wear the suit."

I jokingly scowled. "I prefer casual myself."

"Well, I'd hate to get bloodstains on this. Dry cleaning is expensive."

"Tell me about it." I chuckled. "Do you know the cost of getting necro-blood out of most fabric?"

He caught the waitress's eye and called her over, then shook his head at my question.

"More than it costs to kill them," I continued.

"Sounds like excellent margins," he said sarcastically, with a grin.

"They are. Also, the reason I wear black."

"Thought that was cause of your goth friend dictating your shopping habits."

"Partly that." I feigned exasperation but couldn't help a subsequent smile.

The waitress arrived. I ordered black coffee and Colin ordered coffee with a bit of milk.

"So," he started, as the waitress left to fulfil our order. "What got you into monster hunting? Not judging, but it isn't the most traditional of part-time jobs."

"Well," I hesitated. Wasn't really a conversation for a date on my end. What do I tell him? That I lost my parents, went borderline insane, met a knight from another realm and then realised I liked stabbing things? Yeah, that'd go down well. "Let's just say I really don't like monsters."

"Good a reason as any."

"I must say…" I noticed that I was fidgeting with a paper sugar sachet. At least I wasn't playing with my demanzite sachet. A lot of casters took exception to having those in the same room as them. Kinda like waving a loaded gun around. "You've really gotten better at speaking. No offence."

What the hell, Kat? I yelled at myself.

Despite my immediate regret at the statement, his face lit up. Not the reaction I'd expect pointing out his old stutter.

"You really think so?"

"Yeah, definitely." I smiled, relieved that he hadn't taken offence. "Talking to you after the court case, it was like I was speaking to an entirely different person."

"Hopefully, a more appealing person…" He made a face that was a cross between a boyish grin and light flirtation. I couldn't help but laugh.

"That flirting?"

He blushed but laughed too.

"I ironed out the stuttering pretty quickly. Public prosecutor got me a lot more cases after that and it was good speech practice. And, got to admit…that was my first case."

"Really?"

He raised his hands, almost defensively. "I know, I know. I'm sorry for risking your neck on my inexperience."

"No, no," I shook my head. "You were great."

"Really?" He sounded almost nervous. Like a dog desiring affirmation. Was cute. In a sheepish way.

"Well, I got off, didn't I?"

"Hah. You did, didn't you?"

The coffee arrived. While we drank, we discussed some of his cases, some of my hunts and why he became a lawyer. Unlike me, he didn't have some personal violent vendetta. Neither was it about the money. The law was a genuine and peaceful passion for him. So much so that while he spoke to me, I could see him looking past me. His eyes glazed over, and he spoke in detail about his relationship with his discipline and why it mattered.

"Never thought that much about the law," I said in response to his explanation of how the law kept the Council in check and on the straight and narrow. "I always considered the law to be the thing keeping me from doing my job properly."

"It does that, sure. But it does more than that. The law can be a tool for good and ill. And it can just be a tool. What it is at the end of the day is an essentially human creation that has ascended past humanity. First, with the rule of law, where we control ourselves with our own creation – enabling society – and then with the literal Spirit of the Law, which keeps Hope City from devolving into lawlessness or dictatorship. The law is a fine balance between control and freedom. It is walking that line that I love so much about my career."

Colin didn't stutter once during his explanations. Neither did he sound nervous. He sounded like a man with a passion. It was honestly quite appealing, and it helped me forget all my teenage angst and uncertainty at this rendezvous. Drinking coffee with someone with such passion and knowledge was worth it even if nothing else came out of this.

As was a common trope in my life, however, Colin was interrupted by the barely muffled screams of people just next door. Without thinking, I knocked over my chair in my hurry to stand up. Colin stood as well, but with more grace.

The screaming rose in volume and pitch. I listened closely. It had to be next door. The fast-food place, most likely. I tried to distinguish between human screams and other sounds. Besides rapid footfalls and the usual cacophony of human-made chaos, I could not hear the cause of the commotion.

"What is it?" Colin asked, noticing my thinking face.

"I don't know..." I replied, my voice cold and professional now. It was the type of voice that often chased people away. I almost kicked myself, but then noticed that Colin didn't seem shaken by it.

"A monster?" he offered.

"Maybe. I'm going in."

I expected some sort of argument, or at least some indication of discomfort. I could not help but recall my first date with Andy, which had been interrupted before it started by the mimic, and my blood-soaked dress. Rather than do anything that I expected, Colin nodded, sternly.

"I'll back you up."

Back me up? I looked him up and down. Suit and tie. Expensive dry-cleaning. His hands were clenched, but he wasn't shaking. I looked at his face. He was serious.

I nodded. "Let's go."

Colin threw some money at the waitress as we ran out. I had already drawn my knife – a medieval style dagger called a seax. It was sharp and hardy but wasn't comparable to my now lonely dusack short sword. I hoped it'd be enough.

People who weren't scattering in every direction, pale as sheets and covered in other people's blood, were milling about the entrance of the fast-food joint, trying to take a look inside. Cops hadn't arrived. Of course, they wouldn't. Even when I was being called in after the fact, I tended to arrive faster than the cops.

"What is it?" I asked a bystander, the only guy who didn't look like he was about to vomit up his lunch and breakfast.

"Some sorta monster," he said, a quiver to his voice.

"What kind of monster?"

I must have been as scary as said monster, as the man flinched. I rolled my eyes. Colin touched the man's shoulder.

"We need to know what we're up against."

The man looked at Colin's hand on his shoulder and then visibly calmed.

"I don't know. But it was not like any sort of undead you see on the news. I think it is a spirit. Some people ran right through it."

Just my luck. Spirits were bad enough to get rid of with the right equipment, but a spirit that was killing people and me with none of my exorcism gear...

"We'll need silver if this is a spirit. May be a wraith."

Colin nodded. He looked confident in my prognosis. He shouldn't be. I'd never fought a wraith before. I only knew a bit about them. Mostly that they were probably the most dangerous spirit you could run into.

"There's people still in there!" a woman screamed. I looked through the glass door. I couldn't see any monster, but the floor was covered in blood and dismembered corpses. A young man and woman were crouched behind the cash counter. They looked like they'd seen a ghost. I suspected they'd seen much worse.

I gritted my teeth. I needed to go and get silver, but what if I took too long? I watched the pool of blood on the tiled floor grow ever larger, seeping into the cracks and staining the white tiles red.

"Kat," Colin said. "I'll go find some silver."

I looked at him, a bit shocked. I'd forgotten he was there. I shook myself out of my despairing reverie.

"I need any silver you can get. It is the only thing that can make contact with ethereal flesh."

Colin nodded and, without further hesitation, ran back into Café Henna. That left me with what I did best. Hunting, and trying not to die.

I muscled past some bystanders, seemingly paralysed with fear, and shoved the glass door open. It was quiet inside and the outside world became muffled when the door closed behind me. Right now, I wished that I'd memorised some purification spells. More and more, wizardry would be helping me not get myself killed. That was ignoring all these weird instinctual purification spells I'd been incanting these days. Couldn't rely on those, though. A wraith could spit me while my brain was still figuring out I was in danger.

I heard a squelch as I stepped forward. I looked down. Thank Athena that I wasn't squeamish! The thing I'd stepped on looked like it might have been a lump of flesh in better days. Now, it looked like something an indie horror film director would use. It was disturbing how cheap real life special effects often looked.

"I don't see anything," Treth said. He was obviously talking about the monster. Not what it had left behind. I fought the undead for a living and seldom did I ever come across scenes like this.

I took a step forward, ignoring the squelching, wet, stickiness underneath my feet. The living staff behind the counter poked their heads out. I stopped and motioned to my eyes. The staff were as white as snow. The man ignored me and just stared. Shock. The woman was not much better but glanced to the side. That was all the warning I needed.

I dove forward as a roiling mass of spectral skulls, spikes and blades tore the air where I'd been standing a moment before. I sprang up from my new position and turned around to examine my assailant.

For something that was a spirit, it looked pretty solid. It hovered above the ground and wore torn, black drapes over a malformed body. Underneath an equally torn hood, its face peeked out – if I could even call it a face. It looked like someone had given a metal skull three long fangs and then squished it into a mask. This was no mask though. It was floating just in front of the rest of its body, and I could see nothing behind it. Most menacing of all, however, was its two arms, bearing claws as long and as sharp as swords, dripping with blood.

It stared at me unblinkingly, twitching its sword-like fingers in minor spasms. Its black drapes shifted sharply and unnaturally. As if there was something roiling underneath.

It fit the description of a wraith, but the descriptions could not do it justice. Waves of pure anger and malice emanated from the creature. Its every move was one of either calculated extreme violence, or the catatonic twitches of a highly distressed beast.

The main question was: how was I going to defeat it?

In a silent flash, it was before me. I ducked just in time as it raked the air, slashing a few strands of hair off my head. Hopefully, it wouldn't be noticeable. And hopefully, I'd be alive to care that it was noticeable after this was all done.

I slashed towards it and felt only cold. An intense icy shock shot up my arm and I almost dropped the knife. This was not my type of prey.

"Run!" I yelled. The woman showed indications of doing so, but the man remained still. I bit my lip in frustration, dove underneath the wraith as it attacked my last position and ran towards the far end of the room. The wraith considered me with its dead, hollow lack of eyes. I felt a bead of sweat run down my forehead.

Where was Colin? Where was the silver I needed? And what the hell was I doing here? Was I even getting paid to do this?

The wraith twisted its head and looked straight at the staffers behind the counter. The woman flinched and fell backwards.

Without hesitation, I charged forward as the wraith turned towards its new prey. Along the way, I sheathed my knife and grabbed a plastic food tray. Wraiths could only be hurt by enchantment or silver, but they were still semi-physical. That meant that I could still block their path. With only a moment left before the wraith's blade-fingers made contact with the stunned man, I felt just a bit of pressure as I knocked the creature's hand out of the way using the tray. Even through the plastic, I received the chill that had shocked me earlier. I let out a squeal and dropped the tray. The wraith considered me for a second, and then drove its claw through my skull.

At least, that's what it intended. I only moved my head at the last moment and lost only a bit of my scalp, the blade glancing off the side of my skull. I already felt the blood pooling over my ear. I caught a glimpse of my own blood and flesh matted hair flick off the wraith's blades.

I stared at it, racking my brain for a solution. A way out of this. The wraith brought back its claws, and I realised that I had no solution. I prepared my body for another evasion, knowing all too well that the wraith had me pinned.

Black smoke rose from the wraith's back and it let out a shrill and head-piercing wail. I saw a silver dessert knife embed itself in the creatures back. It wasn't a clean stab, but it was good enough. I rolled and found myself standing next to Colin, carrying a plastic bag of silverware.

"Sorry I'm late," he said, passing me the bag.

I felt the air sting the injured side of my scalp. I'd need to spend a chunk-load of my savings to get that healed. Would probably need to accept the Citadel's payment. So much for honour and principles.

The wraith ceased its scream and twisted its head on its body to stare right at us. I dipped my hand into the plastic bag and brought out a collection of silver cutlery and even a silver-plated watch. I threw the stack at the wraith. It recoiled at the blow, black smoke bellowed from welts opening in its ethereal and monstrous flesh. It was hurting, but I knew it wouldn't be enough. Wraiths were hardy spirits, even against silver. I took out a silver plate and passed the bag back to Colin.

"Keep it stunned."

He nodded and took more silver projectiles out to throw. I tested the edge of the plate. It wasn't sharp, but it'd do.

Colin let out a volley of silverware and I charged. Even in its painful throes, the wraith managed to scrape my shoulder, adding another cut to the jacket and another scar on my already scarred upper arm. I didn't stop. With two hands, I brought the plate above my head and then swung down on the wraith's skull. I made contact and the silver dented, yet I felt no resistance. I swung again from the side and felt the same. No resistance, as if hitting only air, but a dent appeared. Only the fact that the wraith wasn't slicing me indicated that I was doing something right. I swung again, and again, until the plate was twisted and morphed into a little ball. The wraith had shrunk down with every blow, until it was the size of a child, floating meekly just above the ground. I drew my knife and held its point against the now malformed silver plate. The wraith's skull face was on the other side. Like driving a nail with a hammer, I used the sharp pressure of the knife to insert the last bit of silver into the wraith's spectral being.

It burst into a puff of black smoke. There was silence and I felt the intense pain of my head injury start to ignite in earnest as I panted out my adrenaline.

"So, when's the next date?" Colin asked, panting just a bit himself.

I bit my lip and then burst out laughing.

Chapter 13.Party

Colin had been a literal lifesaver with the silverware. It had taken him some legal wrangling and (admittedly) quite a bit of lying about bylaws to get the stuff, but the point was that he got it. The reward from the City was good enough to cover reimbursing the owners. I offered Colin a cut, as was professionally expected. He graciously declined. I used the rest of the pay to contribute to my medical expenses. Was going to leave two scars, but my hair would be able to grow over the head cut. In the meanwhile, I wore my hair to the side to cover some unflattering stitches. Well, shouldn't complain. It could have been much, much worse. Even so, I spent a lot longer in front of the mirror tying my hair just right so that most of the stitches would be covered.

Conrad didn't give me much time to recover. While he was upset with me for delaying the payment from the Titan mages, there were still monsters to hunt.

So, that brought me to a revenant, stalking people by the fens of Lakeside. Had never fought one before, but it was still my cup of tea. All rotting flesh, sinewy, with bones sticking out of it. Revenants were undead. Typically, undead which had been dead for a long time. Think of them like zombies, but a lot more rotten and a lot angrier because of it. This revenant had stuck its hand out of an old grave lot. Some freak necromantic ritual from miles away hit it and rose someone's grandpa or grandma from the grave. Couldn't really tell which. It didn't look human anymore. Lucky for me and the residents, it also lacked a pair of particularly human limbs – legs. When necromancers brought revenants from the dead, they tended to use their powers to enhance the body parts that were left. Not with this specimen. It was as rotting and as cadaverous as the day before it started screaming.

I found the thing crawling along the ground, scraping itself along the grass by the lakes and swampy marshland of the Lakeside suburb. Was easy to find. People were watching it from afar, as if it was a distant car accident or a street performer. I made my irritation known as I walked past the crowd of onlookers, considered the hissing, gurgling and stinking wretch before me, and then skewered its head.

The crowd dispersed sluggishly. There was an air of disappointment about them as I snapped a picture of the revenant and watched my pay get deposited into my account.

"I think they wanted more of a show," Treth commented. I heard distaste in his tone. My sentiments exactly.

We travelled in relative silence back home. I managed to hitch a ride back with one of Hope City's rare buses. Much cheaper than a taxi. I really needed to get a car or bike...

In the almost empty bus, I could not help but feel a tad melancholic. It didn't help that the sun was considering setting, turning a blue sky and yellow light to a more sombre orange and red. This melancholy grew. What was the cause?

Was it the revenant? Did its pathetic form trigger some sympathy in my cold and battered heart?

Can't be. I'd seen much worse. I'd done much worse. I felt the same about the revenant that I did about all undead. At best, a cold indifference. At worst, a vehement hatred.

What I was feeling had nothing to do with the revenant.

Was it, then, worry about something happening in my life? I did not know what. Things were going fine, relatively. I was on good terms with Trudie again, I was chatting with Colin online every night, my bank balance was good. Duer had cleaned my apartment's weyline so well that Pranish even asked to come visit so he could enchant stuff using the local magic supply.

Life was, as far as I could tell, pretty good. Just needed to wrap up this business with the Citadel. I'd come to my senses and agree to be paid eventually.

The bus stopped in Rondebosch and I got out to walk the rest of the way. My bag of gear felt oddly heavy on my back. I'd put my sword in it. My lonely sword. Really needed to go get another one.

The street leading up to my apartment building was quiet, as usual. I heard some birds tweet at a cat. It wouldn't be Alex. He didn't like leaving my apartment. The local cats were mean.

I arrived at the foot of the stairway leading up to my floor and let out a heavy sigh.

"Happy birthday, Kat," Treth said, quietly.

Yeah, that was it.

I scaled the stairs and came face to face with my apartment door. I messed with my keys and then opened the door.

"Surprise!" bellowed out of the door like a shotgun blast. I would have jumped if I hadn't been stunned.

Trudie came running towards me, holding Alex. She was wearing a dark red and grey plaid skirt with black knee-high socks.

"Happy birthday!" she squealed, evidently more excited about my traditional rotation around the sun than I was. Alex meowed at me as I reached to stroke him.

I looked past Trudie's shoulder into my apartment. Behind her was a motley crew I'd never expect to congregate in one place. A bunch of people from so many different parts of my life I'd forgotten they were from the same city.

Just behind Trudie was Pranish, beaming like he used to. Andy stood next to him, with his friend from Miriam's party. And speaking about Miriam, there she was, wearing her vampire black petticoat. Next to her was Brett, Guy and even Cindy. And to top it all off, there was Colin, wearing a casual t-shirt and jeans that made him looks years younger.

So many people. So many parts of my life.

"Don't cry," Treth said, more to himself than to me. He had the start of a sob in his tone.

"How?" I asked Trudie, who beamed at the question.

"When I fixed your phone, I may have given myself access to your contacts. I invited the top contacted people."

She frowned. "Most didn't respond."

That was to be expected. Most of my contacts were temporary clients whom I hadn't even met.

"Most contacted?" I asked, ignoring the blatant invasion of my privacy. "Where's Conrad then?"

"Your smarmy boss is going to meet up with us later at the Gravekeeper."

I smiled. "Got this all worked out then?"

Trudie smiled ear to ear. "Yep."

Trudie cajoled me into the room. I shut the door behind me and put my bag down in its usual spot. My guests started to hustle in to greet me and, in an unconscious daze, I greeted everyone.

"Happy birthday, Katty," Brett teased.

"Surprised you?" Guy added with an almost childlike grin.

Cindy hugged and simply said, "Happy birthday."

"I thought it was only fair I attend one of your parties," Miriam said. I called her prof. She grinned and rebuked me.

Before I could get to Colin, Trudie wrangled Andy and his friend into my way. I looked at Trudie's smile and decided to be polite.

"You remember Oliver?" Andy asked, his too-white smile shining.

I looked at the young man. He had an arrogant grin on his face. Very similar to the one he had at Miriam's party.

"I do." I put out my hand. He shook it. His grip was strong. Stronger than he looked.

"How's the monster hunting going?" Oliver asked, a hint of mockery in his tone.

"Very well. How's the IT?"

"IT?"

It was sudden, and very subtle, but I caught Andy glaring at his friend. Oliver flinched, even more subtly, and continued.

"Ah, IT! Yeah, it's been going well."

"We're aiming on a workable build by next year," Andy added, straight-faced.

What was that all about?

"Workable build? What you developing?" I asked, only a bit curious. I looked over Andy's shoulder. Colin smiled and inclined his drink at me. He was showing that he wasn't offended. I felt a pang that I couldn't explain.

"Video games," Oliver replied.

Andy elbowed him in the ribs and replied himself. "Boring stuff. Accounting software."

"Oh," I said in a barely cloaked tone of forced interest. "Accounting software can be very interesting."

"You should talk to Pranish, babe," Trudie said. "He's developing some sorta magic-code."

Pranish, from across the room, speaking to Cindy, looked our way at the sound of his name. I got the impression he wouldn't want to talk to Andy about his project.

My phone rang before anyone else could speak.

"Ignore it. It's your birthday!" Trudie said, less naggy and more excited.

I smiled, faintly, but still retrieved my phone from my pocket. The caller ID read: Mandy Caleb. My aunt. My last surviving relative.

I ignored Trudie and answered.

"Happy birthday, Kat!"

"Mandy!" I answered with unrestrained joy. I seldom ever heard from my aunt, living all the way in New Zealand. I may be a cold girl a lot of the time, but I really did love my last family member. "Thank you for calling! Isn't it like 6am there?"

"5am. But no matter. It isn't every day that your niece turns twenty."

Twenty. Hadn't really thought about that. Made me feel...old.

I made my way through the party and to my room, where I shut the door for some privacy and quiet.

"Mandy...how've things been?" I asked, almost sombrely. I needed the privacy for more than just the quiet. I really had missed my aunt.

"It's been...well, not going to lie. Have you been following the news?"

"All we hear about here is uprisings in the Zulu empire and Councillor scandals. What's happening?"

"Negotiations broke down," she said, simply, yet with a tone charged with anger and a strong hint of sadness.

Mandy was a mediator for the New Zealand human government and the Sintari elves that had established their own nation on the once human-dominated islands. If negotiations had broken down, that meant she'd failed.

"I'm sorry…" I said. I did not know what else to say.

"Anyway," she said in a slightly more energetic tone. "Let's not discuss that anymore. It's your birthday! What have you been doing?"

I winced. Mandy didn't know I was a monster hunter. A part of me didn't want her to know.

"You know…"

"Hanging out with friends? I heard voices."

"Yeah," I answered, relieved. "Trudie organised a surprise party."

"That girl is a good friend. Send her my best." Her voice had a hint of finality in it.

"You going?" I asked, my disappointment showing.

"I'm sorry, Kat. I have to sort some stuff out. I hope you enjoy the rest of your birthday. Love you."

"I love you too."

She hung up.

I leaned against the door, my cell phone still in my hand. I rubbed my nose and felt moisture pooling around my eyes.

Don't cry, Kat, I told myself. *Don't you dare cry.*

"She really does love you," Treth said.

I knew that. That wasn't the problem.

"I miss her, Treth."

And them.

"Shots!" Trudie shouted, banging the door into me from behind. The door hit the side of my head. The injured side.

"Ow!" I cried out.

Concern flickered across Trudie's face, but as it was obvious I was still alive and well, she showed me a bottle of clear liquid.

"Shots!" she shouted again.

"The sun is still up."

"Pfft...barely. Come through. It's your party."

She turned, and I rubbed my eyes one last time.

"Enjoy yourself," Treth said. There was a hidden message in the statement. *Enjoy yourself because you can.*

I followed my friend back into my tiny living room. Trudie had lined up shot glasses (someone else's, not mine) and started filling them with vodka.

I sidled up next to Colin.

"Happy birthday," he whispered.

I smiled.

"So, I don't have any cake," Trudie said. "But we all know Kat would rather have noodles than cake."

Pranish snorted, loudly.

"But what I do have is a lot of honey vodka…"

"Honey vodka?!" a little voice squeaked, as Duer flew down from his bird-house, glowing an exuberant gold indicative of a truly excited pixie.

Colin jumped, just a little. So, did Trudie and Pranish (even though he knew Duer). The others looked at the pixie with intrigue.

"A pixie?" Miriam asked rhetorically. "You keep strange roommates, Drummond."

Duer floated right down to the countertop, alongside an empty shot glass.

Trudie stared at the creature with a blank expression, and Duer stared back with a cocky one.

The staring match continued. And then I burst out laughing.

Trudie looked at me, and then joined in. Duer didn't look amused.

"Come on, Trudie," I said. "Give the guy a drink."

She poured and Duer glowed the strongest gold I'd ever seen him glow.

Trudie played bartender and poured us all shots. I took two with her, another with Brett, and another with Colin. Miriam looked amused but stuck to her red wine. She really did look like a vampire sometimes. Brett even had shots with Duer, with a little help from Guy. I was a bit worried at first. I knew Duer could handle his liquor despite his frame, but I was worried about Brett's view of him. He'd been a member of the Extermination Corps after all. As much as I liked him, he was trained to kill creatures like Duer. But despite my fears, they both devoured their honey vodka in one gulp and spoke animatedly to each other afterwards.

"Brett left the Corps for a reason," Cindy said quietly from my side. She'd noticed I'd been eyeing him from across the room, a beer in my hand.

"I know," I said, but frowned, as I still wasn't sure.

Cindy was drinking some of Miriam's red wine. She turned towards me.

"He's a good man," Cindy added, almost mournfully. I got the impression that she was remembering someone. Not Brett, in particular, but someone else. "He has his scars. We all do. But he survived what caused them."

She turned away. "Others can't say the same."

Pranish sidled up to me as Cindy walked over to talk to Duer.

"What was that about?" he asked.

"Nothing," I lied. Definitely was something. "Anyway, how are you doing?"

"Fine," he said, and even added a faint smile.

"A man never cries in public," Treth said. "Doesn't mean he doesn't want to."

Treth was right. Pranish had seen things that his much more reasonable heart couldn't handle. As the demon on Table Mountain had said, I was already broken. Saving Trudie hadn't cost me any more of my shattered soul. For Pranish, however, it had cost him his innocence.

I moved closer to Pranish.

"It's okay to talk," I said, hush-hush. I hoped I sounded sincere. I wasn't used to this.

Pranish backed away. "I'm fine, Kat. Really. More than fine. My project is coming along well."

"Trudie said so. Magic code?"

"Not exactly." His tone started to become more enthused. "You know how spells are essentially the primal words of the realms, and when uttered or transcribed they can carry power?"

"Sure."

I understood the basics, I promise!

Pranish nodded, satisfied with my answer. "Well, what I'm doing is putting those words onto a computer."

"Hasn't that been done before?"

"In textbooks? Yeah. But virtual spell-words have never retained their power. What I'm doing is different. I'm inserting the spells into the code of programs themselves."

My blank stare prompted him to gesture wildly.

"I'm making magic software, Kat!"

"Pranish," I said. "I'm not going to pretend to understand all of it, but I don't need to pretend that I'm impressed."

He chuckled. "Well, that's a start."

"Kat-th," Trudie slurred, putting her arm around Pranish, who visibly blushed and tensed at the contact.

"Isn't that one drink too much?" I asked, indicating two shot glasses in her hand. She passed me one.

"One more shot, Kat-thy." She paused to laugh at the word. "And then to the…"

"Gravekeeper," Pranish offered.

"Yes! There."

I downed the shot, while Pranish stole Trudie's and downed hers, and then we all left. I couldn't remember locking my door behind me, yet I could swear I was still at least a bit sober.

***

"Wear it-th!" Trudie shout-slurred.

"Can someone please stop her drinking?" Oliver asked. "She's making a scene."

His grin belied his sentiments. I really wished that someone like Miriam had tagged along to the Gravekeeper instead of him. Unfortunately, she felt a bit too old to engage in such raucous revelry. She wished me luck, reminded me about an assignment due after the break, and then departed. Duer, also, stayed home. Despite his insistent desire to drink more and more honey vodka, he soon passed out. Cindy assured me that he was okay. Pixies got drunk, but it wasn't really dangerous for them.

"Could chug petrol and sleep it off." She chuckled.

I left Duer in his birdhouse, out of Alex's reach. May not even have needed to. Alex was pretty tired after all the fuss and was left dozing on my bed.

The rest of the party arrived at the Gravekeeper. Oliver and a recently sobered Cindy were designated drivers. It was a wonder what healing magic could accomplish! Upon arrival, I was greeted by Conrad, grinning his pearly white grin, and holding up a coat made of scaled hide.

"It's very...orange," Colin commented.

"Wear it-th!" Trudie shouted again, leaning up against Andy. The vodka had already hit her hard.

I examined it more closely, not knowing what to think.

It was, as Colin had so astutely pointed out, very orange. Orange, and scaled. I didn't remember the salamander's hide looking like this when I killed it, but it had been on fire at the time.

"Happy birthday," Conrad said. "I know it isn't a huge fashion item, but it sure is a statement."

"The Spell-Axe carried it off," Cindy said, appearing next to me. She had dropped us off to find a place to park Brett's car. Her words held a venom with enough undertone to write a prequel.

"Cindy," Conrad said. His smile almost wavered. "Good to see you. And you're right. The Spell-Axe, slash Flame Viking, slash Skin Walker, did know how to make it look good."

He looked at me. "And I'm sure you'll be able to as well. Come on, try it on."

I conceded and accepted the orange coat. It was faintly warm to the touch. An effect of it being salamander hide? Fortunately, it felt dry. I imagined that it would feel slimy.

"The scales should be harder than your usual armour," Conrad said.

"Which means better prey for her to catch for you?" Cindy said.

"Better prey for her to catch in general," Brett added. He eyed me up and down. "Nice coat, Katty."

I didn't know what I looked like with it on, but I felt silly. Orange was not anyone's colour. But everyone was starting to settle in, and Conrad looked very pleased with himself. And if it was better than my current armour, who was I to complain?

I smiled, genuinely. "Thanks, Conrad."

"While we're on the topic of gifts," Brett said. "Here's something from me."

He passed me a brown A4 envelope, with the words:

"Happy Birthday, Katty! Love, Brett."

I snorted at the words, but later came to think about them much more intently. I opened the envelope with my seax and read the contents.

"There's a lot of jargon here…"

Colin sidled in next to me and took a look.

"It's from the Ministry of Police. The paperwork needed to…"

He squinted, taking a closer look. The text was very small, and I prided myself on my good eye-sight.

"To register for a firearm license."

He looked at Brett, impressed. "These are almost as hard to get as clearance to scale Table Mountain."

Brett shrugged. "I included a motivational letter and a commendation from an upstanding licensed agency hunter."

"Which hunter?" I asked, stunned by the gift. I'd been needing a gun license for ages. I'd just never had the time, money or connections to get one.

"Me."

"Upstanding?" I grinned.

"I'm as surprised as you are. Anyway, that is most of the hard work done. You just need to find time to go to a station, do your competency test and then sign a few more forms."

"And until then," Trudie butted in. "You can use this."

She was still swaying but had gained a semblance of lucidity. She handed me a rectangular package, covered in Christmas wrapping paper.

"I saw that you have only been carrying one sword these days," she said as I started unwrapping the present. "And, as you have a spare hand…"

The package revealed itself to be a wooden case. I opened it to show a black lacquered sheathe with a tightly woven hilt. A symbol of the Titan's fist dominated the artwork of the square hand-guard.

"A wakizashi!" I cried out, so excited I was about to burst. "How, by the Vortex, did you afford this?"

"Impolite to talk cost at a party," Trudie shushed me. "I got it from a magic shop. Pranish said it was enchanted for hardening or something. Didn't know what that meant, but he said it was cool."

It *was* cool. A hardening enchantment helped keep the blade sharp, strong and tempered. In the past, I hadn't wanted to buy Japanese blades because they struggle to keep an edge but, with a hardening enchantment, that was no longer a problem.

I wrapped my arms around my friend, blade sheathed, of course. Trudie staggered, but then returned the hug.

"Thank you," I said, simply. My gratitude was for more than just the sword. By giving it to me, Trudie had truly accepted my way of life. She had decided to support me down my path. That meant more than anything else.

"Hey, don't I get a hug," Brett moaned, with a joking grin.

I shoved him but then gave him a hug as well.

"So," Conrad said. "Let's get this party started. First round on me!"

***

The first round turned to a second round, and then Trudie brought out the shots again. I was speaking to someone…Cindy, I think, but then Trudie jumped at me, chanting:

"Shots! Shots! Shots!"

I did one, and then continued what I was saying.

"So…he…"

"Who?"

"The demon."

"Right."

"He seemed sad that we beat him, but that he couldn't accept his loss."

"Demons are an odd lot," the person who I'm sure was Cindy replied. "They have weird values."

Conrad walked past, talking animatedly to Oliver. Cindy paused and followed Conrad with her stare, sneering. I waited for her to stop staring.

"What's up with that?" I asked.

"With what?"

"Conrad seems to like you. Why don't you like him?"

"Conrad likes everyone. That's kinda the problem."

"Lilian?"

"Exactly."

"Can't blame him for that," I tried to argue, despite an increasing haze. "He's desperate for cash. Can't vet everyone properly."

"He makes and made plenty off his hunters."

"Why does he live out of his Golf then?"

Cindy shrugged. "Bad credit. I don't know. It's just...Conrad was my introduction to this city. I made all my friends through him. He introduced me to this world."

"He mentored you?"

Cindy nodded.

"Then why the hate?"

"Cause he was a bad mentor."

"I wouldn't say that."

Cindy snorted.

"Well, he produced you, didn't he?"

"Flattery won't get you anywhere on this topic."

"Hah. Fair enough. Well, as long as you don't decide to shift his organs around."

"I'm a healer!" Cindy exclaimed, almost offended.

"And healing can turn to meddling very quickly."

Before Cindy could retort, Trudie arrived again, calling for more shots.

***

"You doing okay?" I asked Colin, who was sitting off to the side, a beer in his hand.

"I am," he said. "A bit soberer than most. Your friend, Trudie, has mercifully skipped me on her shot rounds."

"Want me to call her over?" I asked, slurring just a bit. I wasn't that drunk. Promise!

"No, no. It's fine." He smiled, faintly. "Enjoying your birthday?"

"Yeah," I said. And then more quietly. "Thanks for coming."

"Of course. Why wouldn't I?"

"I don't know, um. Well, shit…"

I felt Treth's embarrassment.

"Shit what?"

I burst out laughing. Colin smiled and took a swig of beer.

"That guy over there?" he asked, quietly.

I looked to where he was looking, pointing nonchalantly with his bottle, as if tipping it into his mouth. Andy.

"Andy," I hissed. I had my head on Colin's shoulder. I didn't remember putting it there.

"You don't like him?"

My aggressive silence was answer enough.

"He keeps glaring at us."

"He's an asshole."

"He looks…jealous."

I lifted my head and looked at Colin's expression. He had a satisfied grin on his face.

"He's dating my best friend," I said. "He better not be fucking jealous."

"Hmmm," Colin sounded, and took another swig. He did not sound convinced.

We sat in silence, and I found my head drifting to his shoulder once again. I noted that this involuntary action was getting on my nerves, even while I didn't mind the results.

"Anyway," I said, hushed. "It doesn't matter what he thinks. I can like who I like."

"And who do you like?" Colin asked, a mixture of lawyering and flirtation.

"You, I think," I said, unthinking.

"Hey, bro," Guy interjected, coming up to the bench holding two pool cues. "Up for some pool?"

Colin looked at me, as if for permission. I moved my head and smiled, giving a voiceless: Go for it!

Trudie arrived seconds after with more shots.

***

I was out of breath after dancing arm in arm with Conrad and Cindy, who were laughing together like (drunk) old friends. I said something incomprehensible to them and left the dance floor. I staggered to where I saw my friend, Pranish, leaning on him for support.

"Having fun?" I asked, a little bit too loudly.

"Yeah," he smiled, but even in my drunken stupor (that I'd deny if you asked me outright), I detected an insincerity. He was staring across the room. I looked at his target.

Trudie, and Andy, laughing together. I looked back at my friend and realised the stare was not just that, but a pointed glare, seeping sadness.

I leaned in and whispered. "You like Trudie, don't you?"

"That obvious?" he said, his words dripping resentment and venom.

I stared back at my best friend and her new boyfriend. "I don't like this."

"Not up to us to like it. If Andy makes her happy, then that's what matters."

"Fucking bullshit," I swore, loudly. I noted that a few people stared at me, but they soon returned to their own conversations.

Pranish looked at me pointedly and then sighed. Heavily. "What am I supposed to do, Kat? I'm her best friend. *Friend*. We've all been friends since primary school."

"I'm not seeing a valid excuse."

I staggered a bit and Pranish caught me. He continued. "I'm so far in the friend zone I might as well apply for squatter rights."

"Friend zone is your fault."

Pranish snorted. He disagreed.

"You want something," I said, slurring between words. "You need to fucking go for it."

I hiccupped and reached for Pranish's drink. I can't remember what it was. Once I was satisfied with more liquor, I continued.

"You fucking go for it and fuck everything and everyone else. You are what matters…"

I swayed for a bit, while Pranish considered his reply. Before he could respond, however, Trudie returned. You know where I'm going with this.

***

The night was winding down. The music was quieter, and the lights dimmer. Everyone left at the Gravekeeper was drinking. The kitchen had closed hours ago. Guy and Colin were playing their 5th rematch and Cindy had gone home after drunkenly crying together with Conrad. Pranish had called it a night a while back. Oliver had also left but I didn't care about that.

With the shrinking crowd, Brett was left alone. As was the norm with him, he didn't seem to mind. I did, however, and as a dutiful host, I went to talk to him.

"What's…up?" I slurred.

"Not much." He grinned. "Fun party."

I sat down next to him and eyed the expanse of the pub. Guy was sweating profusely near the pool table, as Colin lined up his shot.

"Your boyfriend has put Guy in his place. Haven't been able to beat him in pool for years."

"My boyfriend? Oh, Colin. He's not my boyfriend."

"Oh, so I still have a chance?"

I shoved him, and his grin grew wider.

"How old are you anyway?" I asked.

Brett pouted. "Your goth friend is right. You are impolite."

"Answer the question…Bretty."

Brett laughed. "27."

"Eight…seven years my senior! You're practically ancient."

"Aw, shucks. Thanks."

Colin sank his shot and I remembered something.

"How old were you in the Corps?"

Even in my drunken haze, I noticed Brett become uncomfortable.

"I'm sorry…" I muttered, sobering up just a bit.

"Nah, it's fine. To answer…14 when I joined. 19 when I left."

226

14.

14.

I couldn't wrap my head around that number. I thought I had it rough, fighting monsters starting at 17. I realised what that age meant. Brett, smiling, mocking Brett, had been a child soldier.

"I'm sorry," I repeated, looking down. My drunkenness only enhanced my shame.

Brett surprised me by putting his arm around me and squeezing my shoulder.

"Sorry for what? It's fine, Kat. It's in the past."

Could something like that really stay in the past? There was a long pause before Brett spoke again.

"What's your friend's boyfriend's problem, by the way?"

"Andy?"

I looked up and saw Andy with Trudie across the room. My friend was nuzzling Andy, but Andy was pretending not to be looking my way.

"Fuck if I know."

"He looks jealous."

"So, I've heard."

227

Brett removed his arm and I suddenly felt an intense disappointment. The ending of his warmth left a notable cold patch.

I leaned forward towards the table and rested my head on my hands. Brett left and returned with two more beers.

"Last round," he said. I took one sip and then stopped.

"I don't understand," I said.

"Don't understand what?"

"Relationships."

"Pfft. That makes two of us."

***

Someone dropped me off at home. I don't know who. Last I remembered, we were all drunk as…actually, I'm too drunk to think of a simile. Whoever it was, they escorted me to my door, waited for me to let myself in and then left.

My apartment was dark. Should have left some lights on. I was sure I did but could have been drunk enough to have forgotten.

"Enjoy your night?" Treth asked. His question was sincere, as far as I could tell, but there was a hint of displeasure in his voice.

"Yeah," I said, not moderating my volume despite the late hour. I recalled reading a 4 or even 5 on the car's digital clock. "What's up?"

"Nothing, nothing. Colin is nice."

"Yeah," I said, raising my eyebrow quizzically. I staggered my way to the bathroom, using the wall to hold myself up. "So is Brett."

I don't know why I added that last part. Maybe because of the reaction I felt from Treth.

I expected some sort of lecture. Instead, I got a sigh.

"What is it with you and Brett?" I asked, trying to find the doorknob of the bathroom in the dark.

"Nothing."

"Bullshit."

"Crass."

I sent a glare his way. He felt it.

"Colin is just more...gentlemanly. Competent. You should date him."

"You're not my boss."

I didn't mind the idea of dating Colin at all but having Treth tell me to do so riled me up in all the wrong ways.

229

I somehow opened the door and went in. The light switch didn't work. I thought nothing of it. I was too used to the dark.

"I don't want you to be hurt, Kat," Treth finally said, stopping me in my tracks.

"How would Brett hurt me?" I asked, hushed.

"The same way I could hurt you. Because we are broken. And scars don't need more scars. They need bandages."

"I'm a scar?"

Treth ignored my question. "Brett walks a dark path. He'll be lost, in the end, and you will suffer for it."

"We walk the same dark path, Treth."

Treth didn't respond.

I gave up on trying to find my toothbrush in the dark and left.

"Anyway, Treth, Colin is more my age. It will work…"

I stopped.

It was dark, but in the darkness, I stared through my window, curtains drawn. Two jet-black eyes stared back.

Chapter 14. Creeps

I sobered up immediately. Adrenaline and fear can do that to you. And while I did not consciously realise either, I felt the latter very much, as the pair of unblinking eyes stared at me from the other side of the glass. The eyes were unmoving. Only a glint of moisture, that could have very well been my imagination, made me think that the two black orbs were eyes at all.

My vision adjusted to the darkness and I noted that it was very quiet. I could not even hear the distant traffic of the freeway – normally never ending. I also noted that I was keeping my mind on anything other than the creature attached to my window, unblinking and unceasingly looking at me.

"What…" I finally broke the silence, a quaver to my voice. "Is that?"

"I don't know." Treth hid his fear a bit better, but I felt it. It was like the pang in the heart you usually feel when you're afraid, but externalised.

The creature was a sickly white, like plaster pulled over smooth flesh. Its gait was ape-like, with long arms and legs. Its elongated snout looked like a baboon's, yet I saw no teeth or opening for its mouth. Wisps of dark hair fell off its head like tiny rivulets. Two shiny stone-like eyes held a sense of malicious intelligence as it stared through my window. It clung to my window like a gecko, unmoving. Like one of those sculptures that you swore was following your every move.

I'd call it creepy, but that was an understatement. It was damn well nerve wracking, and I wrestled with vampires and walking corpses for a living.

"Kat," I heard a meek whisper.

"Duer?" I whispered back, instinctively. I didn't feel any more noise would matter. This thing was staring right at me already.

"Don't go outside."

I looked around but couldn't see Duer's glow. A pixie's glow was linked to their mood. If he was not glowing at all, then he must be hurt, or so terrified that he may as well be hurt.

"Do you know what it is?" I asked, looking for my pixie friend. I found him keening underneath a coffee mug. I'd seen almost dead nightlights glow more intensely than my normally exuberant and self-assured friend.

"A curse, Kat. A curse from the void. Ye angered someone, Kat. Someone has sent the cursed void-creepers," he muttered, avoiding my eyes. His accent strengthened when he was stressed.

"What are they?" I asked again. Angered someone? Couldn't begin to think who. Long list. And most of them were dead.

He looked at me, and I felt the terror in his gaze. "Creatures from the In Between. They do not move through our world, Kat. But they can still hurt us."

I touched my friend's shoulder lightly with my finger. He was shivering. He must have experience with these void-creepers. And by his reaction, it must not have been a good experience.

I looked at the creature. I had not seen it move, but its head had swivelled towards me, watching. I shivered.

"Why isn't it coming inside?"

"It hasn't been invited," Duer said.

"Ah, like vampires in the old myths?"

Duer did not respond. But I got the gist. While real vampires didn't need to be invited inside someone's home, many demons did. While I couldn't be sure, this creature on my window looked to be nature defying enough to be a demon of some sort.

I moved to lean back but felt a tug on my finger. Duer was grabbing me.

"Don't go, Kat," he pleaded.

I frowned. Could I not go? Did I have a choice? There was a monster, or even monsters, besieging my home. I needed to leave eventually. And it wasn't just that. Mrs Ndlovu and the other residents were outside. The monster, or monsters, couldn't come into my apartment, but they could just as easily kill anyone walking past. Even if I was their target, they were still beasts. Collateral damage was their *MO*.

I retrieved my cell from my jeans pocket. My new salamander-hide coat was faintly warm as I touched it. Maybe I could get over the orange. It was comfortable. Snug.

My phone was dead. Not just out of batteries. It smelled burnt. The same way it had smelled after the demon on the mountain had attacked me the first time. Was he around here somewhere? It was possible. He had not disappeared as a result of his defeat. Even if nobody else had died at the Citadel, I was sure he was still out there.

"Power's out. Phone's dead," I muttered. "Any ideas?"

"Ask Duer if they can survive sunlight. Maybe they are more linked to the old vampire myths than just the rule of invitation?"

"Duer," I asked, with as quiet and as unthreatening a voice as I could muster. "Can these things survive the sun?"

Duer looked up at me. Thought for a second. "No, but they cannot die either. They disappear back into the In Between during the day."

Cannot die. Great…

"Sounds like we need to wait," Treth said.

I thought for a second and then nodded. "I don't like it. Would rather fight it. But if I can't see it move…"

I looked at the creature again and swore that one of its three elongated fingers had changed position.

"If I can't see it move, then I'm just gonna need to wait and figure this out in the morning."

And I had an assignment due tomorrow. Ugh. Well, was either going to be hungover or dealing with cursed demons. This was a more poetic option for the likes of me.

"Can anything hurt them?" I asked. Duer didn't answer.

"Duer?"

"You talking to me or yourself?"

"You."

"I...I think I saw one bleed when we were going through."

"Through what."

"I don't know."

I groaned.

"No use, Kat. He's hard to speak to at the best of times," Treth said, trying to be the voice of reason.

I went to sit on my couch, but with the creature looking right in on me, I stopped and decided to sit on the stool by my kitchen counter. I knocked over some glasses. Didn't hear them crash, though. Would need to clean up the place – when this was all sorted out.

"If I must fight them, and I can't see them move, then I must just anticipate where they're heading."

"Hopefully, you won't need to."

"Better to have a plan just in case."

Treth grunted his assent.

I sat in the dark, staring at the thing staring back at me, in silence for what seemed an age.

"Kat, go get some rest. It can't come in."

But how could I sleep knowing such a thing was just a few arms' lengths away? And how could I sleep knowing that someone, or something, wanted me dead.

I could not. So, I sat, looking at my quarry with eyes wide open, until the nightly dark outside began to abate, just a bit, and I could see the creature more clearly.

"Morning is almost here," I said.

"And you haven't slept a wink," Treth commented, in a voice much like Trudie's nagging.

Duer was snoring. He'd finally fallen asleep, curled up in a mug.

"It should disappear soon. Hopefully, no one will coax it into violence before then."

As if by some sick twist of fate, I heard a door open, and someone start whistling. It was from the floor below. Mrs Ndlovu. I was sure of it.

The creature did not move. I watched it, as still as a statue. I watched the light approach, slowly blanketing the outside with indirect illumination. Yet, the creature did not disappear. It must still consider it night, then. I'd also still consider this night. If given the choice, I'd be sleeping at this time. This thing didn't give me a choice.

I heard feet scale the stairs. The volume of the whistling increased. I heard a thud, thud, thud. Silence. The silence lengthened. A woman gasped.

I involuntarily glanced towards my doorway and, when I looked back, the creature was gone from my window.

"Fuck!"

"Kat, don't do anything stupid."

I ignored him and dove for my new sword. Whoever had escorted me in last night during my stupor had left it next to my bag, with my dusack. I drew both and pulled the door open.

Nothing but the tweeting of birds and the revving of morning traffic. It was light now.

"Mrs Ndlovu?" I called out.

No reply.

I could have sworn I heard her.

"Anyone?"

No reply.

Was it sleep deprivation? Did I imagine it?

"You did hear something, right?"

"I did."

Treth didn't get sleep deprived. Someone had gasped outside here. Someone who couldn't reply.

"It must be day now, right?"

Treth didn't answer.

I gulped, held my swords in a defensive posture to defend my flanks and took a step forward. And another.

Nothing. No Mrs Ndlovu. No person at all. Not even a corpse.

I sighed in relief. It was not impossible that both Treth and I were delusional. I turned to go back inside my room and found myself staring into two jet-black eyes.

My swords didn't hit anything, but something dug deeply into my thigh and I cried out, falling to my knees.

"Behind!" Treth shouted, genuine panic in his voice.

I stabbed behind with my dusack but made no contact. Something bit down hard on my injured scalp. I flailed my wakizashi in its direction and it stopped.

I caught glimpses of its plaster-white flesh and unnaturally black eyes but couldn't see it clearly. It kept moving. Teleporting, or whatever it was doing with this *In Between* nonsense that Duer was on about. How could I anticipate where it was going next? It could go anywhere, it seemed. And faster than I could react. I felt blood coating my outer-thigh and on the side of my head.

A blow to the back of my head sent me reeling and my vision shook. I tried to lift myself off the ground but could only manage rolling out of the way, narrowly avoiding the creeper landing just where I was. I stabbed in a random direction. Made no contact. Felt something skewer my shoulder.

I gritted my teeth. I didn't want Ndlovu coming out and risking her neck. If someone was to die, it should only be me.

The creature disappeared and I felt a temporary relief. That was broken as I saw it on the roof above me, its head craned down, staring without any hint of human emotion. Passionless. Unfeeling.

I lifted both my swords up above me. My hands shivered as exhaustion and pain wracked my body.

It disappeared, and I closed my eyes.

An intense heat emanated from me and I opened my eyes. I was on fire. Well, not me. But my coat, at least. I was still lying down, and an inferno that felt as pleasantly warm as a campfire was bursting out from my salamander coat. It now looked like the beast I'd killed to get it. More than that. It was unleashing an inferno far deadlier than anything that lizard had put out. I felt that the fire should have scorched me to a crisp, yet I felt only an agreeable warmth within the coat.

The fire abated and I stood up, slowly. Dark red was spreading through my jeans and I felt pain in my shoulder where the thing had tried to pierce through my armour. It didn't feel stabbed, though. Just bruised. All in all, I was in better shape than the monster.

"Duer said it couldn't die," I rasped between panting. My vision blurred.

"Duer is often wrong."

The creep was an emaciated burnt crisp. A black skeleton that could have been excused as a modern art exhibit.

"Seems this coat is useful after all."

"Kat…"

I was about to ask why he sounded so frightened and then I collapsed.

Chapter 15. Morning Light

I woke up where I'd fallen, only moments later. Feverish. In intense pain. But I knew I had to get up. So, I did. I'd let myself recover later.

The burnt-out husk of the creature from the In Between was gone without a trace. Seems Duer was right. They couldn't die.

The sun was beating down hard through the cracks of the apartment building and its neighbouring towers. It was blessedly daytime and the creature, or creatures, would give me a breather. As I stood, I winced at the pain in my thigh, my shoulder, my scalp. Everywhere.

"You need to rest," Treth begged. I pulled myself along the handrailing of the stairway. Down, down, down onto street level.

"Someone wants me dead," I rasped.

"Don't help them then."

I didn't know if he felt my pain, but he should detect my anxiety.

I passed Mrs Ndlovu's residence. Her lights were off. I remembered that it was Sunday. Mrs Ndlovu would be sleeping in. Then, who was it that I heard?

I felt a cold chill mix with the pain. I'd been tricked so easily by the creature. I'd have to be careful. But what if it really had been Mrs Ndlovu? I shivered. I didn't want to think about it.

I got to the bottom floor of my building and noticed that I'd spilt blood all over the handrailing. My shoulder was bleeding, dripping blood from my arm, to my hand. It was now all over the usually white painted metal handrailings. I hoped Mrs Ndlovu wouldn't be too mad. I'd clean it up when I was better. When this was finished. I had a lot of cleaning up to do after this was done.

For now, I needed help. And if these creatures were of the demonic variety, there was only one person I'd trust. Said person would also be able to heal my wounds, and better yet, remove the curse.

I limped my way to the top of my street where, by a new art-shop, there was a very old payphone. Practically ancient. I hoped it would work. My cell was still fried. I gripped onto the side of the payphone booth, breathed heavily to stave off the pain, and fished in my pocket for coins. I had a few. They weren't dollars. Only digital transactions (which most were) used dollars in Hope City. For physical transactions, people still used the old Rands, from when this was still Cape Town, and still South Africa. I inserted a few coins, not counting, and then dialled Cindy's number. At least what I thought was her number. It was miraculous the clarity that trauma could bring. Through the heat of agony, I could remember things I normally never could.

"Hello?" Cindy groaned. She sounded hungover. I'm sure most of the attendees of my party last night were, at least a little.

"Cindy," I rasped, meekly. My vision blurred at the exertion of speaking. I was looking down, resting my head on the payphone. My jeans were dark with blood.

"Kat?" Cindy's voice cleared up immediately. "Where are you? What has happened?"

"Corner…of…my…"

I almost ripped the phone off the hook as I collapsed. I saw black.

***

I'd like to say that I fought through the pain and exhaustion, and that I stoically found help myself. But this is not that sort of story. I lay prostrate on the ground, on a Sunday morning, on a street where nobody helped me. I awoke in Cindy's car, lying on her backseat. I passed out moments later.

When I woke up again, Cindy was above me, her forehead creased, skin pale and hands glowing gold. I felt an intense warmth on my thigh and only the echo of pain on my scalp and shoulder. I felt epochs better, but Cindy looked like she was on the verge of being undead.

"Cindy," I acknowledged, my voice still weak. My throat was dry.

"Don't move," she said. Her voice was still strong, despite the sickly pallor to her skin and the hollowness of her eyes. This magic must be taking a lot out of her. It would. Healing mages normally only stopped someone from dying and then let the body and medicine heal the rest. Cindy was going further. She was helping me recover fully.

"Stop," I managed to croak out. "You're killing yourself."

Cindy did stop, but only after there was no more pain and only its memory.

I sat up, and she sat down, sinking into an armchair. I was in a place I didn't recognise. It must be Cindy's home. It was utilitarian. Soft colours. Very few decorations.

Nothing gaudy. The only hint of extravagance was a wall covered in photographs and another covered in spell glyphs.

Cindy rubbed her temples and then looked at me. I was sitting on a medical bed in her living room. Odd as that may be, it somehow fit into the room.

"What happened?" Cindy asked, simply.

"Duer, the pixie, said I've been cursed."

"I detected a curse. What form did it take?"

"A creature. A creepy white thing that was stuck to my window but couldn't enter without an invitation. Duer said it came from the *In Between,* whatever that is."

"The *In Between*?" Cindy pondered. She glanced at the photos and I saw a hint of sadness, for just a moment. "This creature. Did it move faster than you could see?"

"Yes. Do you know what it is?"

Cindy nodded, grimly. "I do. We called them void-creeps. Or just creeps. They infest the realm between realms. The half-world. What many call the In Between and others call the Void. Yet, they come from another realm. A demonic plane called the Undying Woods. A realm of endless darkness and innumerable dead trees that were never alive in the first place. It is home to a wind that

246

emanates from nowhere and only serves to lead its victims into eternal travel and torment."

"How do you know all this?" I asked, rubbing my thigh. I felt the tingle of new flesh, but no more pain.

"Because, I went there."

"Went there?" I asked, dully. Can't blame me. No Earth-born human had left Earth and returned. Much less one that had survived a demonic realm.

She nodded. "Only for a moment, but it was enough. There, I found the dreadful scenes of the battle-dead, strewn across the black and husky soil, frozen in the throes of the trauma that had caused them to have their souls flung to such a place. Many were from realms of which we have no knowledge. Others were more recognisable. Those wearing the bloodied French and German uniforms of Verdun, emaciated figures from the gas chambers of 20th century Europe, the war-weary and crushed spirits of Stalingrad and the ancient yet still suffering souls of Marathon. They were frozen in time, yet still forced to suffer every waking moment of their demise."

"How...how did you escape?"

"The man with many names. I called him Tom."

I looked at the photos more carefully, and saw a bearded man wearing a bright-orange duster. The Flame Viking, the Spell-Axe, the Skin-Walker. Tom.

"You've been cursed with a demon homing beacon. The creatures of the In Between, who have fed so long on the trauma of warriors, will hunt you in the darkness…until you are no more."

Cindy said this with a sense of resignation. If Cindy was giving up, what hope did I have?

"You can remove the curse, right? A purification?"

She shook her head. "I cannot. This isn't some spurious curse flung by an uppity corruption mage. Someone got your blood and your true name."

My vision blurred, and my heart threatened to pound out of my chest.

My true name?

True names were the last defence of a mortal from magical destruction. They were the most closely guarded secret of any person. If someone knew my true name, they were practically holding a loaded gun to my head. Worse!

"But, you aren't defenceless against the creeps," Cindy said, and stood up so suddenly that I almost jumped. She disappeared out of the room and then returned.

"I saw that Brett is teaching you how to shoot."

She handed me a small wooden box. I accepted it and flipped open the lid to reveal an old-fashioned pistol, with a varnished wooden handle and deep-black metal finish. The pistol was linked to a silver chain, draped across the wood-chip supports within the box. Its barrel was long, jutting from a small box internal magazine. I recognised it from some old war game I'd played with Trudie. I wasn't a military historian, but I could approximate the era. End of the 19th century or early 20th century.

"World War One?"

"Just over a decade out. Boer War. The second. It is a C96 Mauser Pistol. Its official designation is the *Die Weltreisepistole des Dreiunddreißigsten Reiches*. But call it Voidshot."

I examined the weapon closely. German was stamped on the side of the body. I only understood the date. 1896. Three years before the start of the Second Boer War.

"This weapon found itself in South Africa, so far from home, in a time of bleak turmoil and violence. It became a part of this violence, as such was its function. So much so, that it was imprinted onto the Undying Woods. As warriors find themselves doomed to forever lie dying in that dark world, so do their weapons. This weapon, however, escaped. It travelled with us through the In Between and returned to Earth. After that, it gained an unusual ability. It could fire its rounds, no matter how previously conventional, through the realm between realms – damaging those who were hit. Usually, the residents of the void know no fear of our conventional weapons. The pain and suffering of Earth cannot follow them into their dimension. But, bullets fired from this gun can."

I examined the weapon closer. It looked normal to me. I gripped the broomstick handle.

"I don't have my license yet," I said.

"Since when has the law ever stopped you?" Cindy said, the hint of a smile on her lips.

I stood up and Cindy passed me a leather holster. I attached it to the back of my belt, where my coat would conceal it.

Cindy handed me a stripper-clip filled with silver tipped bullets. I accepted it and she showed me how to load. I holstered the pistol and attached its chain to my belt. Hopefully, I would be able to draw it in time. Hopefully, it wouldn't come to that.

"Thanks, Cindy," I said. "For everything."

"Survive, Kat. That's all I ask. They are compelled by a master to hunt you. Slay the one who placed the curse and the creeps will lose interest. "

I nodded. I knew what I had to do.

Chapter 16. Faith

One would expect a full parking lot near a church on a Sunday morning. Not in Hope City. Christianity had taken a knock worldwide since the Cataclysm. In Europe and South America, it still survived through an evolution of its key functions (turning to purification, the pursuit of magic and the understanding of the Seraphim), but the traditionalists of Southern Africa couldn't keep up with the times. As people flocked to the Titan Cult and secularity, the Church suffered.

As I stood outside the thick double doors of this old chapel, I could not help but feel intense discomfort. I had not set foot inside a church since my parents died. Struggled to subscribe to the same world vision after that. Few could.

I took a deep breath, smelling the morning moisture and the wood varnish from the door. At least I was moving around. Cindy had expended a lot of her spark to heal me up, so I could pursue my curser. It meant she couldn't aid me, but beggars can't be choosers.

I cricked my neck and pushed both doors open. A gust of wind from inside sent my coat aflutter.

The church was empty. No congregants. Yet, it was not in ill-repair. Every pew looked freshly waxed, every stained glass window dusted and every candle lit. There was not a soul in sight. I hoped that the man I was looking for still worked here. It had been a while. But it was my only lead.

I took a seat in the second row from the altar and looked up at the statue of the Virgin Mary. I couldn't help but grimace. I'd been a good Catholic girl for eight years. Now? Religion and I didn't get along. Try going through what I've gone through and seeing what I've seen and maintaining a good relationship with faith.

I sat quietly for quite a while. Treth was silent, examining the room. I wondered if the chapels on his world looked anything like this.

Finally, a door opened in front, and a man wearing a black priest blazer and white clerical collar appeared. He was old. Greying everywhere he could grey. He had been old when I saw him last. And that was an age ago.

The priest was reading from a book while walking but did a double-take when he saw me. It must not have only been that he wasn't expecting company in this society that was bored of church. I must have been quite the sight, with a quarter of my hair shaved away, my scalp stitched up, wearing a flaming orange coat, with the pommels of two swords sticking up from my backpack.

"Child," he said, with the croak of age. "How can I help you?"

Child? I thought the scars made me look at least a bit older.

"Father Digby," I said. "You may not remember me, but my family used to come here for mass."

He squinted at me, deep in thought. I recognised the look. It was the same one he had when answering questions when my family and I came here. He hadn't seemed to have changed a bit.

"Drummond?" He asked.

I nodded. So, he remembered me.

He nodded, satisfied. "You have your mother's eyes."

I felt an uncomfortable sensation. I didn't like him mentioning my mother.

"Father, I sadly don't have a lot of time. I have some questions."

He sat down at the end of the pew and looked at me. Worry lines criss-crossed his already wrinkled forehead.

"Of course. Speak, child. Once a part of my congregation, always a part. I have missed your family during my sermons. I am so sorry about what happened to them. A dreadful thing to happen to a child."

Yes, dreadful.

"Father, you know my true name. Correct?" I ignored his statements.

A look of brief shock. He didn't expect that question.

"Yes...yes. Your parents wanted you christened in the manner set forth by Pope John Paul II in 1998. Children of the Church were to be granted their true names with an ordained minister as witness. I do recall your name. But I will not utter it."

"Thank you, Father. I appreciate the silence in this regard. But it may be too late. Someone, or something, has gained knowledge of my true name. As my parents are dead, you are the only other person with knowledge of my true name."

"I would never use your name to do you harm," he said. His tone was sincere,but I was in a mistrustful mood. But I had to keep acting civilly. As much as it hurt me to do so.

"Slow and steady," Treth said. "I know you're anxious. But we're close."

Treth always knew when he needed to remind me to behave. Was almost irksome.

"Do you believe in God, Ms Drummond?" Father Digby asked suddenly.

I considered the question, initially shocked, but then shook my head.

"I believe in gods, but not God."

He looked disappointed as he stood up and clasped his hands behind his back.

"A pity. But to be expected. Very few youth of this Cataclysmic age have faith. Why look towards the heavens when the marvels are here on Earth?"

That wasn't my reasoning, but I let him continue.

"One would think that magic and its wonder would be testament enough to God's miracles. Let alone the existence of his adversaries and servants."

"The Seraphim have rejected their allegiance to a god," I said. It was a well-known fact. The Archangel Michael of the Seraphim, when conversing with the current Pope Gabriel I, stated that the angelic hosts followed each other's wills and their own. They had no knowledge of a greater power."

"Many reject God's role on Earth. The angels have revealed themselves to be as ignorant as we are of these matters. Immortality, disappointingly, does not bring wisdom. There may be a God that created both the Seraphim and us. But like us, the angels do not know. They are blind to truth and can only be saved by faith."

I resisted rolling my eyes. I needed to get to the point. The clock was ticking.

"Father, sorry to speed this along, but I have limited time. Someone has put a curse on me using my blood and true name. The curse summons demons to hunt me at night. I have until sunset to find the culprit."

"And do what?" he asked.

I hesitated.

"Kill them?" he suggested. He shook his head. "A shame what has happened to you. Rachel would be sad to see you now."

"Don't talk about my mother," I hissed, almost yelling. I realised my volume and quietened. "Please..."

Digby looked at me with accusatory, yet pitying, eyes.

"You walk a dark path, Katherine. But it is your path, now. I will help you. You say you are beset by demons?"

I nodded.

"One thing to come from the Cataclysm was an enhancement of our understanding of God's enemies. All demons are a part of a hierarchy. Servants to another. Hell is not a purely chaotic place. Oh, no. It is structured. Regimented. Every demon has obligations, rules and fealty."

I nodded. I knew this all already.

"At the top are the Archdemons, who lead their own hosts to achieve their twisted agendas. Every demon owes fealty to an archdemon eventually."

He placed his hand on the top of the pew and looked at me grimly.

"Whatever demon is after you, a greater demon pulls its strings. And true names are no obstacles of these demons. They know our names. They can get our blood. And they can summon hordes to beset us mortals."

Digby's voice slowly faded away as the pieces started connecting.

Cindy had been called in to hunt an archdemon that escaped. The Titan mages started dying around the same time. And the demon who claimed to have done it knew my name.

Just my luck. To get rid of this curse, I'd need to slay an archdemon.

***

"Conrad," I said into a disposable cell phone I bought from a corner shop.

"Kat? I've been trying to call you! New lead on your pet Necromancer."

New lead? No, have to focus.

"Phone was busted. I'm cursed. Void-creeps after me. Have to kill their summoner. I think it's the archdemon from the mountain. The one who was killing the Titan mages."

I was talking fast, rapid-firing all my points over the phone while speed-walking back to my apartment.

"Whoah, whoah. Calm down. Are you hurt?"

"Not anymore. Cindy saved me."

"Good old Cindy. Where are you?"

"Pinelands. Walking back."

"Long walk. Why do you think it is the demon? I thought you got rid of him."

"I told you that I didn't."

"I was hopeful. So, what hunches do you have?"

"Someone got my true name. Archdemons can apparently do that. Only living person who also knows my true name is an old priest with no magic to his name. So that leaves the demon from the mountain. He's the only being that I know who has the capacity to get the stuff needed to curse me. He also has motive."

"You think he summoned the creeps?"

"Who else could it be?"

"Kat," Conrad said, hesitantly. "Demons, even archdemons, can't summon other demons. Demons require a mortal tether. A human summoner."

"What?" I stopped in my tracks. I'd seen the entire puzzle complete, but now I realised I was missing half of it. Digby had been wrong, and that was my only lead. Wrong, or lying. "So, a human wants me dead?"

"Looks that way. Who did you piss off?"

"Long list, but none of them demonologists."

"Void-creeps only come out at night. You've got a few hours."

"And I should be finishing my assignment. Ugh, will have to give them a curse-note."

"I'm sure Miriam will understand. Anyway, got a client to talk to. Good luck and keep me posted."

He hung up and I was all alone on this street, hours until demons were gonna come out and renew their hunt for my flesh.

"So, someone wants me dead."

"Someone has wanted you dead before," Treth responded.

"Yeah." I pictured Jeremiah Cox's mutilated face lying in a pool of his own blood. "Didn't work out for him."

"We'll pull through this, Kat."

I nodded. "But how?"

"Connect the dots. Just because the archdemon can't summon demons himself doesn't mean he isn't connected to all of this. Remember what he said. He is currently being controlled by someone else. Perhaps, his summoner is the same person who cursed you?"

"You're getting good at this, Treth."

"We're getting a lot of practice. The question is: who is the summoner?"

I stopped underneath the shade of a tree and thought. Who would want me dead? Who, with the capacity to summon demons? Not just demons – an archdemon.

Demon summoning took extremely powerful sorcerers. They needed all that spark to keep the demons in line, or risk becoming demonic fodder. So, that meant someone with a big spark pool, or an incredibly talented wizard who could find a substitute for their own lack of spark.

There were no corpses of the missing Titan mages. Only blood. But blood could be falsified in this age of magic. Cloned and sprayed over the place of the 'murder'. And if people thought the mage was murdered, nobody would go after them if they were abducted.

A sorcerer's spark was a raw power source but, with a skilled enough wizard, it could be turned into something reminiscent of a very powerful weyline.

I got home by the time I had figured it all out. Or at least thought I'd figured it all out.

It was simple, as things often were in hindsight.

They had my name. They could have gotten that from my run-in with the demon. They had my blood. Easy to get in my line of work. But who had the motivation to abduct sorcerers? And who would have the raw desire for vengeance to take these sorcerers from the Titan Citadel?

It was late by the time I got home. The sun was setting. I was running out of time. I phoned Conrad. Before he could speak, I asked.

"Do you still live in your car?"

"Why?" he asked, defensively and just a bit embarrassed.

"The void-creeps aren't allowed to enter a home without permission. I think I know who set the demons on me. I just need a lift. Preferably a lift which the demons won't be able to rip through."

Hesitant silence. Then…

"Okay. I'll come right over."

I went into my apartment, ignored the clutter from the party and the empty spot where the creep had been last night, and changed my clothes. My old clothes were still sticky and stained with blood. I put on my full monster hunting gear. Thicker denims, with lots of pockets, a t-shirt topped with a polymer vest, my face-plate, greaves, arm-guards, gloves. And to top it all off, my new coat. I checked my blades for nicks. The dusack had a small one. I hadn't had the opportunity to test the wakizashi's hardened edge yet. Lastly, I checked Voidshot. Its safety was on. Its chain shimmered as I clasped it. Would I need to use it? Could I use it?

I put out some food for Alex and was just about to leave when Duer flew down onto my shoulder.

"I want to help," he said.

"How?" I asked, finding my keys.

"I can detect the creepers. I can warn you."

That would be useful. I gave him my voiceless assent and locked the door. I noted that my blood from earlier had been cleaned up. Would need to apologise to Mrs Ndlovu later. But, for now, Conrad was parked just outside.

Chapter 17. Revelation

"Why do you need to go to the Titan Citadel?" Conrad asked, screeching through traffic and racing against the setting sun.

"Suspicions."

"I hope more than suspicion. Our contract is basically up. Will take some wrangling with Whiteshield to let us up."

"I trust you'll be able to pull something out of your hat."

We screeched to a halt just outside of the cable station. A few Whiteshield guards aimed their guns at us, but they recognised me as I got out of the car.

"I need to see the mages," I said in a tone that didn't brook dissent.

He tried anyway. "You no longer have any clearance."

"Hey," Conrad said, still at the wheel. "You a private?"

"Lance Corporal," the guard said.

"Well, lance corporal, you won't be jack-shit if my hunter isn't allowed to get up there. The Citadel is in grave danger and she's the only one who can save them. So, if you like getting paid to stand with your arse against that wall all day, then let her through."

"Sir…"

"Don't *sir* me. Let her pass."

The guard looked at his friend desperately. His friend shrugged.

"Well, she had clearance once. Should be fine."

They let me through. Conrad remained at the bottom, in his car. I suspected he didn't want to be outside it when the creeps arrived.

I didn't note the cable car trip up. I only tapped my fingers impatiently on the hand railing, the sun slowly setting.

"Come on…"

"It will be fine," Treth said again. I felt his anxiety just as much as mine.

The cable car docked and I ran past the Whiteshield and Cult guards towards the Citadel entrance. Duer was jiggling in my front pocket. The front door of the black tower was ajar. I ran through and moved towards the voices.

I burst through a door to the sight of a circle of red-robed mages around a conference table. They stared back at me, questioningly. Some noticed Duer in my front pocket but didn't comment. Stephen reddened with anger and Charlotte raised her eyebrow so high that it disappeared past her fringe.

"Ms Drummond? There are proper ways to come and receive payment…"

"I'm not here for payment," I panted. "The murderer is among you."

"Murderer, Ms Drummond?" Stephen bellowed. "The demon was the murderer, and you extinguished it. Finished. What is this about a murderer?"

I held onto the door frame, making sure not to stab myself on one of the Citadel's odd spikes again, and caught my breath. I really wished that I could level my accusation at Stephen. He deserved to look a bit sheepish in front of his peers and underlings. But facts were more important than my feelings.

"Charlotte," I said. "The night that I complained about no Whiteshield guards to let me off the mountain. Was there really a lockdown? I was told that I could not come in that night due to the Citadel being locked down."

She squinted, thinking. "No, there wasn't. There shouldn't have been, at least."

"Who was on duty at the door at that time?"

"If you are here to criticise our staff, then there are proper channels," Stephen interjected. I ignored him.

"Who was at the desk?" I repeated my question.

"Cornelius," Charlotte replied. "But he may have been in the bathroom. Or the system may have failed."

"He was probably dozing off," a Titan mage muttered. It seemed that not only Stephen disliked the wizarding receptionist. There were many bullies here. That just confirmed one of my suspicions.

"When I first came here, I cut myself on one of these spikes. Cornelius cleaned up the blood."

"So?" Stephen said.

"I have a curse on me, Meister. A curse that requires my true name and blood."

"And you suspect Cornelius?"

Did I? Poor, bullied, Cornelius. I liked him. But, the evidence all pointed towards him.

"He had my blood."

"And your true name?"

"He could have gotten that from the archdemon."

"Archdemon? I thought it was just a demon."

"An archdemon of unknown identity escaped Heiligeslicht last month. Around the same time that Titan mages started disappearing."

"Disappearances which have now halted."

"For now. But I suspect that's only because they know I'm onto them. They are waiting for me to leave the picture and then they will renew their abductions."

"Abductions?"

"Cornelius is a wizard," I said, resisting a sigh. How could they not see any of this? "A wizard requires an external power source, as you probably remind him constantly. The archdemon was summoned in Pinelands. A light weyline. If a being of such power was summoned in a light weyline, someone would have noticed the weyline darkening before the ritual was even complete."

"Are you suggesting that Cornelius, our Cornelius, summoned an archdemon?" a Titan mage asked, amused.

I looked him dead in the eyes and said. "Yes, I am. And more than that, I am suggesting that the disappeared mages have been abducted by Cornelius, who used his understanding of surveillance and manipulating footage using magic in order to hide the crime."

There was a brief silence.

"I was meant to die, but the archdemon had other plans, as demons often do. Now, Cornelius seeks to finish the job using demons designed to assassinate."

"These…" Stephen hesitated. "Are strong accusations. But worth exploring. Charlotte, where is Cornelius now?"

"He should be manning the desk."

"He wasn't there when I came in."

"How did you enter?" Charlotte asked.

"The door was open."

Charlotte stood up with a hurried anxiety. "The door was what?"

"Cornelius is gone, I presume," Stephen sighed. "If this wasn't evidence enough, then his fleeing his post is."

Charlotte rushed past me, seemingly more anxious about the door than the escape of Cornelius. I followed her.

"When did the meeting start? How long ago did you see him?"

"Not long. Five, maybe eight, minutes."

He could not have gotten far. There was one way up and down.

"Sergeant," Charlotte called into her radio, examining the ajar door of the Citadel. "Sergeant?"

"No answer?"

"Fucking Whiteshield. The Council pays them a fortune and they are never there when we need them."

"He's probably gone down the cable car. I can catch him at the bottom."

"Go," Charlotte said with finality. I did so.

I ran towards the cable station and hurriedly told the Whiteshield guards to let me down. The sun was only just peaking out over the horizon.

"Can you do it?" Treth asked me, when in the confines of the cable car.

"Do what?"

"Kill Cornelius."

"I don't have a choice."

He couldn't argue. This time, I didn't.

It was dark when I reached the bottom cable station. Only the white, clinical lights of the station provided some sort of beacon in the growing sea of darkness. No Whiteshield guard greeted me. As I entered the foyer, I saw why.

They were dead. All of them. The sergeant who had tried to stop me from bringing my swords to the peak. The arrogant smirking sorcerer. All of them. Their faces were torn into terrified expressions of rigor mortis. Some had no visible wounds. Others had dark ligatures around their necks – strangled. Others were missing their intestines. Blood pooled on the smooth floors, collecting at the base of the Titan's fist.

"Kat, they're here," Duer whispered.

I drew Voidshot. The click of its safety echoed in the silent hall. Still. Silence. I couldn't even hear the cars on the nearby roadway. No sound, but I saw it.

The white statuesque, ape-like creature with black-stone eyes. It hung upside down above the front door, staring at me. This time, there was no glass between us.

I took aim. It didn't move. I didn't fire.

A bead of sweat slipped down my forehead and onto my cheek. Every moment I wasted, Cornelius was getting away.

"Behind you," Duer said.

I fired Voidshot over my shoulder and turned. The bang set off ringing in my ears. The recoil wasn't as bad as Brett's 9mm, but still shocked my arm. The creep over the door had disappeared. A chunk of its white flesh, stained by black blood and ash, was left behind.

"Thanks, Duer."

"There're more outside."

"I know."

I exited the building to the sight of a slaughter. Whiteshield guards lay dead, everywhere. The guy whom Conrad had bullied had a bullet in his head. I had no way of knowing if it was friendly fire or Cornelius' handiwork.

But that concern was the least of my problems.

White ape-like demons were staring at me, hundreds of them, clinging from lamp posts, the walls and other adjacent buildings. They were quiet. I was not sure they could make a sound. None of them moved. Well, I wouldn't be able to tell if they could.

"Kat? Get in!" Conrad shouted, opening the door to his car. I bolted in. A creep dove in after me, but I managed to let loose a round into its head, before it popped out of existence. I closed the car door.

"Good fucking Zeus," Conrad swore, covering his ears. "There's a reason I fired Brick. Too many misfires indoors. Tinnitus treatment is expensive."

"No time! Did you see a robed Titan mage come this way?"

"Yeah. He looked like he was ready for a stroll. Probably dead like the rest of these poor souls. Couldn't even let them in. These monsters appeared in an instant and started killing everyone. Our friend guard over there got pegged by his own comrade in the chaos."

I looked through the windscreen. Creeps were already clinging to it and the passenger window. I was going to have nightmares after this was all over. Or maybe I wouldn't. If I finished this, I may have already overcome the fear.

"Step on it! We need to catch that mage. He's responsible for all of this."

Conrad revved the engine without hesitation and sped off, swerving to knock off the creeps. Some fell but reappeared soon after. I considered firing a round through the windscreen but thought better of it.

We drove down the mountain track, faint lampposts and the car headlights to illuminate our path. The black eyes stared unblinking. I kept Voidshot drawn and my other hand on the hilt of my sword.

I needed more time. More time to interrogate Cornelius. To ask why. To find out where he was keeping the mages. To see if he was truly evil or just a victim pushed too far. I needed time. But I had none. All I knew was that this man was running from me, and I had to chase him.

"Is that him?" Conrad asked, peering through the legs of the creeps.

I saw the back of a red-robed mage, running up a dirt path, obscured by shrubs. He turned his head towards the headlights and I saw the glint of his glasses. Cornelius. The car could not go any further. So, I opened the door while we were still moving, and dove out. A creep exploded on the fire of my coat, but the force knocked the wind out of me. I landed on my knees and fired blindly and wildly, putting three bullets into the air. No creeps pressed further. I ran up the dirt path, after Cornelius.

Cornelius rounded the corner of a rockface and disappeared. I cried out at him. A wordless cry, calling for him to halt.

I turned and saw creeps closing in. They silently and motionlessly covered the dilapidated mountain road, the cliffs and Conrad's car. They did not attack but, with every blink, they moved closer towards me. They must be hesitant now that I was armed with something that could hurt them. But that hesitation would only last so long.

It was properly dark on this side of the mountain. No light from the city to form a fake starfield for my comfort. The glow of my coat was the only thing that lit my way. It was on fire, but I didn't feel its burn. It was as if it had claimed me as its true wearer. I felt a tinge of sadness that I'd killed its real owner. But if I had not, then I would not have the coat now to help me. Life and the hunt were not a morally simple affair.

"Cornelius," I shouted, as I ran up the dirt-path past the bend of the rockface. Creeps pressed in on me, staring unblinkingly. "Cancel the curse. Call them off. Don't make me kill you!"

No response. The path was shrinking, as it became hemmed in by a sheer cliff and an unguarded drop down the rest of the mountain. I wasn't really afraid of heights, but anyone with half a brain would feel a bit of acidity in their stomach as they stared down the dark abyss. My footing was shaky on the path and I had to move with my back to the wall, skirting along the edge. I looked up and saw beady black eyes staring down at me.

"Cornelius!" I shouted again. I saw creeps clinging to the cliff above me. I fired but saw no evidence of any death. "Give up. None of us has to die."

With every step, my heart jumped. I couldn't see far ahead and couldn't get a proper grip on the cliff to steady myself. I kept my hand on Voidshot, levelled in the direction of the creeps, advancing ever closer as I blinked and panted. The path continued to shrink.

How did Cornelius come this way so fast? And why this way? Was it a part of his plan? Was I going into a trap? Or was he simply desperate and ran down the first path he saw?

The path widened and I turned a corner. Ahead, there was a precipice, overlooking the Southern Suburbs of Hope City, looking like a Christmas tree with all its different coloured lights.

On the precipice, Cornelius stood, with his back to me. He was doubled over. Panting. In the silhouette that the city lights formed around his body, I saw the dark shadow of spittle and vomit trail down his chin and onto the rock and dirt below. I suspected now that this was not a part of his plan. That he was not a seasoned killer. He attempted to escape and went down an unknown path, pursued by me as I was pursued by his hunters. He was probably betting that the creeps would get to me first.

"Cornelius," I called. I felt a stab in my back. The coat tried to immolate the assailant but failed. I fell forward and turned my head. Creeps covered the mountainside. A sea of white, with black beady eyes. Their silence was more unnerving than the gurgles and screams of a thousand undead.

"Call them off!" I shouted. Creeps closed in, blinking in and out of existence. They looked impassive, but also a bit curious. I'd already killed a few of their number. But what did that matter? They blanketed the mountainside. I couldn't last forever. Rifts! I wouldn't last a few more seconds.

Cornelius turned to me, and I saw sadness in his eyes. Moisture behind his glasses. A quiver to his lip.

"Kat! They're coming," Duer shouted. My chest constricted, and I lifted my gun.

I tell myself every day, "Never hesitate!"

"Kat!" Treth shouted. I felt the presence of the creatures behind me.

Hesitation is death. Hesitation is the end. Evil doesn't hesitate. It doesn't care.

They were closing in.

But Cornelius, poor Cornelius, stared into my eyes and soul. He was not evil. But he had done evil things. He was just a victim. A man pushed too far.

Could I call that evil? Could I call the victim evil?

No. But I still pulled the trigger.

Chapter 18. Secrets

I never really decided if Cornelius deserved to die. The creeps disappeared as soon as his corpse fell off the mountain. He had summoned them. He had been the murderer. I finally accepted payment from the Citadel, even though I had not found the location of the missing mages. The Citadel helped keep the cops off my back. No vigilante or murder charge like with Jeremiah. The public prosecutor was satisfied with the results. The Citadel, even more so. Not only had the disappearances stopped, but they had someone to blame. Everyone was satisfied. Except me.

More than resentment had pushed Cornelius over the edge, and I needed to find out what. I needed to piece together the last pieces of the puzzle of the man who wanted me dead. I needed to know why.

Charlotte gave me Cornelius' address and, after handing in my assignment late to Miriam, I went to my latest victim's home.

Cornelius lived in a small house in Pinelands, a sleepy suburb locked between the North-Road settlements, Old Town, the Southern Suburbs and the border slums. It was a district of contradictions, which hid all its angst behind the veneer of suburban pretension and make-believe. It was the perfect place to raise a family. But by the size of Cornelius' house, I doubted that he was doing that. Charlotte confirmed my suspicions. Cornelius was, or had been, a bachelor. A hard-working, if side-lined, wizard and administrator.

Charlotte gave me all this info on Cornelius with her usual impassivity, but I did sense a subtle change in her tone, the way she avoided my eyes and the speed at which she wished to get rid of me.

Charlotte, perhaps unlike the rest of the Citadel, had liked Cornelius.

Should that make me regret killing him?

Should that make me sad?

I did not know, and I did not give myself time to find out.

It was late afternoon by the time I found time to visit Cornelius' house. I'd finished Miriam's assignment on theories of vampire contraction compared to lycanthropy, handed it in, had lunch with Trudie, checked up on Pranish in the IT lab, hunted a barghest for Conrad, bought some groceries for myself, Alex and Duer, hunted a few routine zombies, finally bowed to Treth's insistence to eat...

You get the picture. It had taken me awhile to get to Cornelius' house. Now, I stood on the front lawn, my hands in my pockets, scrunching up my salamander coat behind me. The lawn was well manicured. Green. Uniform. I glanced up and down the street. A dog-walker eyed me up and down but looked away as I looked back. I was used to stares. I'd need to get more used to them with my new get-up.

"Be careful, Kat," Treth said.

"I'm just tying up loose ends, Treth," I replied, taking a step onto the grass, towards the tiny home. "No more creeps tailing me."

I felt the echo of pain on my wraith and creep-caused wound on my scalp. I was no longer hiding the scar that covered the side of my head.

"The archdemon..."

"Is gone," I interrupted. "Cornelius must have been the one holding his reins. Makes sense. The demon was summoned in Pinelands. Cornelius lives here. He had a motive and showed a willingness and ability to summon demons to do his dirty work."

"What was his motive, though?"

I frowned. "That's what we're here to find out."

The front door was locked. I looked behind me to see if there were any nosy neighbours. My monster hunter ID could get me out of a lot of trouble, but this still was breaking and entering. Even if the owner of the house was already dead. I may have dodged the murder charge, but that didn't mean I wanted to risk serving another day in court. I'd feel bad about Colin defending me *pro bono* a second time, and I knew he'd do it too.

I held a lockpicking scroll to the door and exerted my will. The paper disintegrated as it tapped into the local weyline and channelled that power into manipulating the door lock. I heard a click and the door was unlocked.

I closed the door behind me quietly. More habit than anything else. I didn't think there'd be anyone, or anything, home.

The first thing I noticed in the orange afternoon light, was a cross on Cornelius' wall. Not the Titan's fist, that I'd expect from an employee of the Titan Citadel, but a crucifix bearing the likeness of Christ hanging from it.

"Cornelius was a Christian, it seems," I said aloud. Very peculiar. It wasn't a normal thing to find a Christian who practiced wizardry. While many churches had reconciled natural sorcerers with God's plan, most denominations still saw wizardry as a sinful corruption of the world. In my opinion, it was just a way for the cardinals who had spark to justify their power while still keeping the little guys weak. Wizardry, like guns centuries before, was the equaliser in this magical society. The naturally powerful didn't like equalisers.

I walked quietly, my sneakers only creaking slightly on the old wooden floor. The cross was by itself on the wall, overlooking the front door like a silent watcher. I reached towards it, but stopped, and turned away.

"Back in the church…" Treth started.

"Would rather not talk about it," I stopped him.

"What did your God do to anger you so?" He ignored me.

Cornelius' living room, just to the right of the front door, was sparse. No TV. Just a single armchair and bookshelf. I squatted down to examine the titles. Nothing theological as I would expect. Nothing magical, even. A motley collection of popular non-fiction titles and a few classics like Dickens and Tolstoy. The types of books you'd expect to find in the shelf of a non-reader who desperately wanted to look like they read.

I read over the same title, not comprehending it again and again. I felt a frustrated anger rise, stemming from Treth's question.

What did my God do?

Nothing. Or something.

And that was the problem.

"He doesn't exist, Treth." I frustratedly sighed, standing up. I had a feeling that the bookshelf wouldn't reveal anything about the nature of the man I'd killed.

"Then why do people venerate him so?"

"Why do people do anything? For easy answers. For a sense of safety. To scapegoat their problems to the unknown."

"Seems that it has to be more than that. On my world, we knew our gods."

"Good for you." I noted that it was getting darker. I hoped that the neighbours wouldn't get suspicious if I turned on a light.

"Not so much. They died before the end," Treth said, sadly.

I snorted. "Gods don't die."

"Perhaps, that is your problem," Treth suggested. "Too strict an idea of what makes a god. For us, it was the virtuous and the powerful. The self-sacrificing beings who kept our society alive, gave life to nature, and kept the darkness at bay."

"And they died?" I asked, my curiosity was sincere, but my tone was irritable.

I felt a sadness come from Treth in the pause. I guessed what he'd say. Much like how Treth had died, and all his comrades, his gods had perished as well. Everything had died on Treth's world. Perhaps, that was why he accepted his lot so readily on Earth. He knew there was nothing to go back to.

"I believed in God, once," I said, eventually, my voice quieter. "But then…you know what happened."

I clenched my fist.

"I cannot believe in, much less worship, a being who created the evil that killed my parents."

When Digby mentioned my mother's name…

"They were good people. They were faithful. Moral."

I checked to see if I was crying. I wasn't. But I should be.

"It got them…"

I shook my head. No use continuing. I whispered, almost spat. "Some mysterious plan."

"I am confused," Treth said. "You speak sometimes as if the God you hate exists, but other times that he doesn't exist. Which is it?"

"Does it matter?"

"No," a deep voice, tinged with casual confidence, chuckled from just behind me. I turned, drawing my wakizashi and dusack instinctively. I noted the comforting weight of Voidshot on my lower back. It wasn't as consoling when I saw the assailant.

He was wearing the same black suit, over a white-dress shirt that highlighted his sharp features. His cleanly shaven face was grinning, underneath a pair of black thumb-sized horns jutting from his black, suave hair. The only difference in his appearance were a pair of obsidian dark, batlike wings, outstretched like an eagle before swooping in on its prey.

I instinctively took a step back. My skin went white and my breath caught in my throat.

His grin grew wider. "Nice coat. A bit bright, but I like how it adds to the ensemble."

He leaned in, half a metre from me. I held my swords out. He ignored them.

"If I may, I advise a black shirt to add contrast. I like *Fleetwood Mac* as much as anyone, but the white overpowers the coat's orange. Perhaps an inverted shirt, with the album picture in white and the shirt in black?"

"What…" I stammered out, simultaneously trying to digest his words. "What are you doing here? I thought…"

"That the creep summoner was my…master? Alas, that is not the case. I am still bound to this world by mortal whims."

He sighed.

"Bound a bit like your knightly companion. I shouldn't be so bitter, though. At least I have my own body."

"You…you know about Treth?"

"Know about him?" the demon chuckled. "I can see him looming over you right now, wearing the same battle-scarred and blackened armour that he wore when he was slain by his own brother."

The demon looked above me, and I felt Treth recoil.

"Do you still love him, Treth Avicin of Concord, Knight-Paladin of the Order of Albin? Do you still love your lich-brother, even after everything he did to you? After he destroyed everything you had?"

The demon's gaze drifted down. Treth was hiding behind me. I felt his breath on my neck. I felt his tears.

"Stop it!" I said, trying to shout. It came out as a whimper.

The demon stared past my shoulder for a few more moments, and then looked me in the eyes. It took all my willpower to return his gaze.

"An appropriate pair," the demon said. "The broken knight, slain by his own undead brother. And the broken huntress, killed in spirit if not in life by the forces of evil."

"I'm not broken yet," I said, tensing my grip on my swords. "And neither is Treth."

The demon eyed us up and down.

"Perhaps," he muttered, as if to himself. "But perhaps not. I see now why my summoner sent me. One who kills the victim so wantonly could just as easily kill the perpetrator. Evil done once, can be done again."

"I'm not evil, demon."

"Really? What would Cornelius think about that? What did he think when he heard the click and bang of your reality-defying gun?"

"He sent the creeps after me. I had no choice."

"Did he?"

"I...don't know. That's why I'm here."

"Then let me expedite your investigation. It is the least I can do after my behaviour last time we met."

He laughed, causing me to jump.

"I'm almost pleased that you had such hidden power. It meant we could have this overdue discussion. Cornelius was not my summoner, as you may now have guessed. But he was working with him. To what ends? I can only begin to imagine the twisted agendas of mortals, but I suspect that Cornelius' goal was similar to my summoner's. The world is one way, and he'd rather it be another."

"He wanted to play god, is what you're saying?"

"Don't you all?" the demon smirked. "Isn't the human paradigm one of twisting nature, thought, and action to suit one's desire? Isn't the entire state of human being a twisting of reality into a fiction that comforts the mortal?"

I shook my head. "I'm not like him, or your summoner."

"Are you not? You pictured a more convenient world where Jeremiah Cox did not exist. You made it happen.

You pictured a world without Cornelius, where his creatures wouldn't pull you into the abyss."

The demon seemed closer, as if he had moved like the creeps. A subtle teleportation.

"You pulled the trigger, Kat Drummond. How does that make you different from them?"

"They…they were trying to kill me."

The demon returned to his spot across the room. He clapped his hands, an uncomfortable sound in the quiet house.

"You figured it out. You did not slay them because they were evil and you good. You killed them because they wanted to kill you. And that is the way of the world. Instigator instigates, instigating others into becoming instigators."

The demon grinned at his own repetition.

"I was not an instigator. They chose their evil ways. That led them to me. I did what I had to."

Why was I arguing with a demon? To be fair, it was all I could do. I couldn't kill him, after all.

"Evil, Kat? You're a smart girl. You should know better. Perspective, and all that. To Cornelius, to Jeremiah, you were enemies. To them, you were evil. You stopped Jeremiah's plan to save people."

"Save people? He wanted to cure disease through undeath."

"And who said that isn't saving people?"

"Me."

"Exactly. But what power do you have to make that true?"

I paused. I couldn't respond.

"You have power, Kat Drummond." I felt an intense authority resonate in his voice as he uttered my name. It was as if my soul had strings and he was strumming them. "Your power is in both your hands right now. You have the power to decide good and evil. But what use are those terms when you can so easily judge them with the point of a sword?"

"It is more than a sword," Treth said. He had some of his strength back. "Good is what serves the righteous. It is what serves the virtuous. Power doesn't determine what is right. It just determines if right wins or not."

"Righteous? Virtuous?" The demon pondered the words. "By whose estimation? God? Can your friend, Sir-

Knight, agree with you? Or must she accept that, without god, there is no right or wrong. What makes good, good?"

"History. The collective stories of human suffering and progress," Treth retorted. "Our gods did not tell us what was right. Our experiences did. We learnt that murder was wrong because of its results. Because of our preferences. We learnt that charity was right, because it made us realise our connection to each other."

"Interesting," the demon said, sincerely. "And something I didn't expect from the uneducated knight of a dead world."

"Treth is wiser than most," I said, feeling I needed to defend my friend. "And he's right. Good is not divinely made. But it does exist. It is what makes being human worth it. It is what gives us, or at least me, meaning."

The demon bowed his head, respectfully. It looked sincere. An acknowledge of a good point. I had not expected it.

"I must thank you. Kat, Treth. I did not expect this discussion to be quite so interesting. I am not entirely convinced. Evil, and good…are all so shaded in grey."

He looked away, as if ashamed.

"But, I may be biased."

He looked at me and I felt raw power emanate from his every limb. His wings seemed to have grown larger.

"It was a good discussion, but it must now end."

I brought my wakizashi up just in time to block his now clawed hand. It didn't break.

"A good toy. Your friend has good taste."

I backed away, ducked under a swipe from his other hand, and thrust forward with my dusack. It glanced off his suit as if I'd been trying to stab solid metal. I felt ringing go up my arm. I hated striking hard objects. Always felt it in the morning.

"Why waste your time?" the demon asked. "Use your power."

What power? The light I used against the vampires, and him? I did not even know if it was my power. Was it even a power?

I rolled away from him. He stared at me and shook his head.

"I was hoping you would be able to fight back," he said. "This is not a fair fight."

"Do you ever have fair fights?" I asked, to delay him as I caught my breath.

"No," he answered, sadly.

He appeared before me in a blur and I was knocked down onto the floor. I felt my insides cave. I spat out blood. My vision darkened, and my every pore cried out. I was dying.

"Treth?" I wheezed. "What do I do?"

He did not reply, but I felt his fear. His shame. The demon looked down at me, his wings crumpled in by the small walls and roof of the house.

"Don't feel ashamed, Treth," I rasped. I felt blood on my chin. "I don't know what to do either."

I felt his tears fall on my cheek, and the warmth of his spectral lap as he cradled me. I'd always thought Treth didn't have a body anymore. I was right, but not completely. He had one, but it lived through me. Through my sensations.

I coughed up blood again. I noted that my hands were empty. The demon looked at my discarded blades and lifted them up. He examined them. There was no hint of his previous smile.

"Go," I said to Treth, through sputters of blood. I didn't know why I said it.

"Where?" he asked. And I saw him. He was sad. Young. Scarred. His armour was blackened with the assault of corruption, rust and blood. His smile was weak, sadder than any weeping.

The demon walked towards us, slowly. Treth looked up at him and drew his spectral sword. He pointed it at the demon, who considered it, before knocking it to one side with the flat of my own blade.

"A sorry pair," the demon said, a hint of shame in his voice. But also...respect.

"Treth," I rasped, looking up at my previously invisible companion with wide eyes. He was not the large, statuesque knight that I'd imagined. He was thin. Almost scrawny. His armour was ill-fitting. His dirty-blonde hair was unkempt and dirty. He looked like a teenager who had been thrust into battle. And that was exactly what he was.

The demon stopped before us. Treth put his arms around me and held me tightly. I couldn't move. I didn't try. The tears came. I couldn't even feel my insides. I only felt Treth's reassuring touch, and his warm tears on my increasingly cold skin.

The demon lifted my swords up. Was as fitting an end as any. I closed my eyes.

Chapter 19. Recovery

I was used to waking up in hospitals. They smelled like medicinal alcohol and musty spell tomes. I was also used to waking up in hospitals in the twilight hours, as the setting sun threw a red tinge on the usually white sheets and tiles of the hospital room. My body clock probably thought it poetic.

I turned my head and saw a box of chocolates and a pile of polystyrene instant noodle containers. Topping it was a letter bearing Trudie's handwriting. There was no one in the room. A private suite. Who was paying for me this time?

"Treth?" I asked. I could no longer see him. I felt a sudden fear that he may be gone.

"Yes?" he replied, and I felt an overwhelming relief.

"What happened?"

"I…I don't know. I woke up yesterday, when we were already in the hospital. Trudie and Pranish have already visited. Conrad and Cindy had an argument."

"Any others?"

"I don't know. What he did to you…it also affected me."

"Did to me? I was sure he'd killed me."

"Seems not."

I heard footsteps on tiles and stopped. I looked towards the doorway to see Andy.

"You awake?" he asked. "I heard you talking to someone."

I looked away. Why him? Why now?

He entered.

"Trudie had to go help her parents with something."

"And you're still here?" I asked, almost spitting.

Calm down, Kat. He's dating your best friend. Be polite.

He sighed and took a seat. I continued looking away.

"What happened, Kat?" he asked.

"A monster," I replied, avoiding eye contact.

"Not that. I mean between us."

"I don't know what you're talking about," I lied.

There was quiet. I contemplated the tree just outside my window. It was getting darker. I hoped someone would turn on my light. I didn't like dark hospital rooms.

"I couldn't help Trudie, Kat. And I'm sorry."

"Sorry means very little to me."

"She's forgiven me. Wasn't even angry. Why won't you?"

I turned to him, and my face must've been a storm cloud, as he flinched. "Because I thought better of you. I thought you were there for me. I thought you were there for her. But you weren't. And you think everything's fine after that?"

His hands tensed on the arms of his chair but loosened. He took a breath before speaking.

"I wish I could explain it to you, Kat. I wish I could tell you everything."

"Why won't you then?"

He shook his head. "Because I cannot. Because you wouldn't understand. Because you'd ki..."

He stopped halfway through the word. Shook his head again.

"The world isn't black and white, Kat. I wanted to help, but I couldn't. Can't you understand that?"

I glared at him.

"Is it that you can't, or that you won't?"

"Does it matter?"

I heard a knock, and Andy stood up. Colin was standing in the doorway. I noted his welcoming smile. And I noted Andy's barely hidden growl and predatory gaze.

"Goodbye, Andy," I said. "Please send my thanks to Trudie."

He looked at me, his growl turning into a sorrowful pout. He walked past Colin, giving him a nod, before disappearing down the hospital hall.

"Hey, Kat," Colin said, advancing into the room, holding flowers and a small box. "How you feeling?"

"Like a demon ripped a hole in my stomach. You?"

"A bit better than that." He took a seat. "These are for you."

He put the flowers (don't ask me what type) in a vase by Trudie's gifts and handed me the box.

I raised my eyebrow and opened it.

"It hadn't arrived in time for your birthday, sadly. But here it is."

It was a silver pocket-watch. Chain and all. There was a card in the box. It read:

"For wraiths. And, so you won't always be too early."

I felt tears well up in my eyes.

"Why?" I asked, shoving down an unbecoming sob. The healers must've given me some weird anaesthetic. Getting all emotional. "It must have cost a fortune."

"Not so much." He shrugged. "And it was worth it just to make that joke."

"Don't tell me you also paid for all this." I indicated the private hospital room.

"I did not, but I did inquire who did. The receptionist said you were dropped off by a man wearing a black suit."

My sudden gasp must have shocked him, as he leaned forward, concerned.

"What is it?"

"The man with the black suit…" I said, shuddering. "He's the one who did this."

"Why?" Colin asked. I saw his hands tense. He probably wanted to punch the demon. I hoped he'd never get the chance. I liked Colin too much for that.

"I was investigating Cornelius' house…the man I killed."

"The man who put a curse on you," Colin reminded me.

"The demon who everyone thought I'd vanquished was there. Mentioned something about Cornelius' motivations. Said he wanted to change the world…"

"And then…?"

"He attacked me, almost reluctantly. That would explain why he took me here afterwards."

"Doesn't explain why he would still attack you, though."

"Demons are odd. They have their own rules, that they don't even follow sometimes. What I'm interested in is what I found in Cornelius' house – and why the demon was sent there to stop me from looking around."

"Did you find anything?" Colin asked, his tone belied his genuine interest.

"I did. A crucifix," I said, after some thinking.

"Cornelius was a Titan mage, wasn't he?"

"Exactly. Which makes the presence of the cross particularly odd."

"Not only that," Colin replied, leaning back and rubbing his chin thoughtfully. "But isn't it a bit incongruous for a Christian to be summoning demons?"

"Very. But even the devil can cite scripture for his own purpose. Conversely, a Christian can use demonology for their own goals."

"Seems a bit heretical to me."

"But maybe not for Cornelius…"

There was silence as we both contemplated what all this meant. What did Cornelius want? Why did he want to kill me? Who summoned the archdemon?

I was sure they were connected. Cornelius wasn't the ring-leader. He was a pawn. But, who was the king?

"The demon said that Cornelius wanted to change the world?" Colin asked.

I nodded.

"Any idea how?"

"I don't know. But, I'm sure he had something to do with the disappearing Titan mages. Oops...wasn't supposed to mention that."

"Your secret is safe with me. Client confidentiality." He winked.

I was still thinking.

"Cornelius wanted to change the world because he didn't like this reality," Treth offered. "Something about this reality."

"A Christian..." I said. "Wearing the robes of a Titan mage. Serving them. Being bullied by them."

"Perhaps, an ulterior motive?" Colin suggested. "Maybe, he was biding his time to sabotage the Titan Cult."

"And risk releasing the Titan?"

Colin shrugged. "Perhaps, the Titan represents the chastened wrath of God?"

"Perhaps...but he seemed saner than that."

"Sanity and insanity come in many different shades. Maybe he's right."

I snorted.

"Well, I'm out of ideas," Colin said.

"So am I. But I think I know who I should meet for more answers. Another Christian, living in the shadow of the Citadel. He might understand what it is like to be a believer in a world bored of miracles."

Colin nodded and stood up. He held my hand and looked me in the eyes.

"Be safe, Kat. Don't do anything stupid."

"I won't." I smiled back.

At least, I'd try not to.

Chapter 20. Left Behind

I was discharged from the healing clinic in the morning, with all my belongings. The doctors and healing mages told me to take it easy. I didn't lie to them. I just didn't say anything other than, "Thank you" and "See you next time."

"Do you really think the priest will have a lead for us?" Treth asked.

I was walking to Digby's church, the warm morning sun on my back. It was nearby and, I felt like the exercise after being bedridden. The marvels of modern magical medicine had me fully recovered, for the most part. It must've been expensive. Healing of this calibre required extreme risk on part of the wizard or astronomical spark usage by a sorcerer.

"He's a priest of a dying religion. The dying religion that Cornelius evidently followed. He may have some insight into what drove Cornelius to act the way he did. Cornelius may even have been a member of his congregation. Not a lot of churches in the area."

I felt Treth's presence as I normally did but could not get his image out of my head. I had seen him. His sadness. His scars. His youth. He didn't fit my expectations but, the experience accomplished so much more. I felt now that my spirit companion was more than just a voice in my head. He was truly my companion. My invisible friend and not merely an imaginary one.

I arrived at Digby's church and took a break in the shade of an oak tree. Despite my refound energy after my healing, I'd still walked a few blocks to get here, during the heat of the day. It didn't help that my coat kept me toastier than normal. I felt I needed to wear it, though. It had a habit of keeping me safe.

"Shouldn't we be in class?" Treth asked, as I listened to the birds. They sounded prettier than usual. Calming. Now that I thought about it, every sound was better than it was before. The wind in the leaves, the distant hum of traffic…

My close brush with death, twice, left me appreciating life. But I couldn't let it change my behaviour. I was too far down this path to stop. Both Treth and me.

"It's nice to be alive," I said, with a sigh, leaning my back against the oak and closing my eyes.

Treth didn't respond.

"Oh, sorry…" I apologised. "Didn't mean it that way."

"No, no. I am just glad you're okay…"

I didn't respond and Treth didn't continue. We sat together in a pleasant half-silence, with only the ambience of the suburb to fill our ears.

Finally, I stood up, groaning just a bit from my post-healing aches.

"Let's go see the priest," I said, unable to hide a bit of discomfort.

"You don't have to," Treth replied. "He probably doesn't know anything."

"He's all we have left in this case. May provide some insight. I need to understand what drove Cornelius to try kill me."

"And who is still trying to kill you?"

I rubbed my chin. "I don't think anyone else is. That demon has had plenty of chances to kill me. But he never does."

"Perhaps the demon is disobedient?"

"Perhaps," I said, with a hint of finality.

I pushed the double-doors open at the same time, unable to resist a dramatic entrance. The wind followed me inside, causing candle flames to flicker.

The church was as quiet as last time. I considered sitting on a pew to wait for Father Digby, but decided to rather stand near the altar, under the statue of the Virgin Mary.

Digby entered as I was contemplating the statue. His face registered surprise for a few seconds, and then changed back to the impassive expression of a man too old to maintain any sort of emotion for long.

"Good morning, Ms Drummond. To what do I owe the pleasure?"

"Morning, Father," I said, still looking up at the statue, only glancing down to register him in my peripheral vision. His hands were clasped behind his back. "I have come with some more questions."

"Answering questions is my job, child. Would you like to take a seat?"

"No, thank you. I have been bedridden for a few days and would prefer to stand."

He nodded, not inquiring why I had been bedridden.

"I...did something that I am still deciding if I should regret," I said, hesitantly.

"Would you like to make a confession?"

I looked at him pointedly. He didn't alter his impassiveness.

"I do not need to confess anything yet, Father. I need to know if it is worth regretting."

"And then?"

"And then I shall seek redemption in my own way…or try to move on."

Digby approached me and put his hand on my shoulder. His touch was uncomfortable, but the coat didn't burn him. That made me let him continue the gesture that must be aimed at comforting a distressed ex-congregant. I reminded myself that, while I may have problems with the religion, I shouldn't have a problem with this man. My parents had liked him.

"Speak, child. Believer or not, you are safe in these halls."

I looked at him, but I couldn't discern anything behind those eyes. I chose to trust him.

"I killed a man, Father, in self-defence. He was attempting to kill me and I had no choice but to take his life to save my own."

"The Lord, much like human law, forgives killing in self-defence."

"I know…but I want…need to know why he wanted to kill me."

He raised his eyebrow, a flicker of emotion. "And you think I can help you understand his motivation? I can only tell you what you probably already know. There are men of wickedness in this world. Monsters in human vessels. There is no reason to their actions. Only malice."

"I don't think this is the case with this man. The reason I come to you is that I discovered that the man is…was…a Christian."

"And you want to understand what could drive a Christian to kill?"

"Not a Christian but, specifically, this Christian. He worked under the Titan Cult but had a crucifix in his house."

"A crucifix doesn't make someone a Christian," he said, a little bit defensively.

"Of course, but it was the only thing that stood out in the house. It was prominently placed and he had nothing else to suggest he was merely a collector. And, he mentioned God before. I didn't think much of it then, but it had a sense of sincerity. I am sure he was a believer."

"And you believe that this may have something to do with why he wanted to kill you?"

I nodded.

He sighed and turned away, taking his hand off my shoulder. I felt a relief at the lack of touch.

"It is difficult to be a man of God in an age of supermen," he stated, as if reciting something he'd been thinking about for a long time. "For some, it drives them crazy. It pushes them to the edge of their faith. Too many go over that edge and forsake their saviour."

I resisted rolling my eyes. This wasn't the type of answer I was hoping for.

Digby turned, as if he'd sensed my irritation.

"You are such a sheep who has strayed from the flock."

"If the flock keeps running off cliffs, it's wise to leave it," I said, just a hint of venom in my voice.

"I understand, Kat," he said. "That you blame God for your parents' deaths."

"I don't," I said, without thinking, but realising that my words were true. "I blame a man. I blame his discipline. I blame the society that allowed him to persist."

I shook my head and continued. "I do not blame God, Father. How can I blame what I don't believe in? God didn't kill my parents. A man did."

His expression, previously emotionless, looked devastated. Would he have looked any happier if I hated God?

"Sorry, Father..." I began, attempting to be diplomatic.

"No, no." He raised his palm to stop me and looked away. "I understand. Atheism is easier these days. It is deemed healthier to blame the here and now, than the cosmic."

"Shouldn't we not blame God at all?" I asked, truly curious. "Even if one believes in him."

He looked at me, a look of incredulity on his face.

"Why?" he asked, simply.

"Well," I said, sheepishly. "Wouldn't it be blasphemy to blame the God you're meant to worship?"

He pondered the question, and then looked at me firmly. "But, child, if God is responsible for an action, should he not hold the blame?"

"Can he not be responsible and blameless?"

"Explain."

"Blame implies wrongdoing. But if God is ineffable, then he cannot fail. Therefore, he might be responsible, but then he cannot be blamed. For there is nothing to blame on him. It went according to plan."

"Even your parents' death?"

I repressed a wince. "No, but that is why I don't believe in your God. I cannot believe that a blameless one can do something which I would so want to blame on them. So, I do not place blame or responsibility with God or his cosmic plan. I place it with the man who murdered my family."

I did not hear the birds chirping behind these thick stone walls. Neither did I hear the traffic nor the wind. I heard the beat of my own heart. My breathing. And the faint echo of my own words inside my head.

Digby, finally, looked down.

"You are right," he whispered. "God, or no God, blame and responsibility rests with man."

I didn't know why it seemed to matter so much to Digby. It was a conclusion I had come to years ago. Do not confuse my atheism with youthful angst. I threw away my faith over a long period of self-doubt and self-loathing. I've fought my battle, and this was my result.

"Kat!" Treth yelled, and I turned down the aisle, to face the archdemon in his black suit.

"Priest," he said, with a juvenile smirk. "Why wouldn't you discuss such interesting topics with me? I could help you realise that you can't place the blame of what you've done on God alone."

I drew Voidshot but as I aimed it at the demon, a magical blast of air knocked it out of my hand. It hung loosely on its chain. Before I could draw my swords, I was pushed backwards into the embrace of the Virgin Mary.

Digby was still looking down, but his fingers were pointing towards me, exuding power.

A sorcerer.

How could I have missed it? Actually, how could I have known? Digby had always been a husk, like me. Like all good Catholics. Magic was playing God. Good Christians didn't play God.

But, I realised, even the most devoted Christian would play God if the way of the world was too obscene for them to allow it to persist.

I tried to speak, but the force of Digby's sorcery threatened to crush my chest. All I managed to accomplish were short wheezes.

"You were meant to kill her," Digby said, simply.

The demon shrugged, hands in his pockets.

Digby sighed, and looked up at me. Or the statue. I'm not sure which.

"I hoped we wouldn't have to have this confrontation, Ms Drummond. I liked your parents. It was a shame that you took a darker path after their deaths."

I felt anger rise at his mentioning of my parents, but I couldn't voice it.

"You asked what made Cornelius do what he did. You wondered why he wanted to kill you. I think, he actually mentioned it to you before…"

Digby came closer, standing just by my feet. I strained to look down at him. My arms were splayed behind the statue. I felt the work of the healers being undone and pain returning to my old wounds.

"The cause," Digby said. "Cornelius' cause. And mine. You asked what could drive a Christian to kill. It was a stupid question. Christians have killed for salvation for all of history. And I do the same."

I managed to wheeze out a single word: "Why?"

"Because…" his face contorted and reddened. No more impassivity. He looked angry. Passionate. And despairing. "When the Vortex came, when the world was rent asunder – that was meant to be the end. To be Armageddon. When hosts of demons attacked our world, the faithful were meant to be risen to Heaven. Then, the forces of Good and Evil would finally clash. A final battle. A final conflict to end the pain of existence."

The archdemon snorted scathingly. Digby ignored him.

"We were…I was meant to rise up. To be raptured, as all good Christians should be. But…I was left behind. I, a faithful servant of the Lord, was denied my place in Heaven. And I had to think what I had done. I pondered this for years. Decades. What had I done? How did I sin? Were my confessions insufficient? Was I wrong? I lost my faith in the Lord. But how can one throw away one's entire life? Their entire world view? I couldn't. I continued to believe that I had done something wrong. That it was not God but I who was wrong. That I had sinned, irredeemably. Only a few – a blessed few – were pure enough to rise-up. I was not among them.

"This thought destroyed me. Almost utterly. How could my God, my all-loving God, abandon me? How could so many, made in his image, be denied? But, finally, I realised what was wrong. Yes, this was Armageddon. The ending of the world. But, it hasn't ended yet."

He paused, staring pointedly into the void.

"The Saviour has not returned. That meant that I still had a chance. The Rapture is still happening. And I have been left on Earth with a purpose. I am to play a role in the upcoming battle. For, if there is to be a battle, there must be an adversary. While the forces of darkness and sin seep into our world, they haven't risen in earnest. Earth has not faced the wholesale destruction yet to require a Saviour. But it must. For, as you said, the responsibility and blame of everything must lie with man. As it is man's role to suffer, it is our role to cause the suffering. And it is our role to cause Armageddon. Only then will God intervene."

I wanted to call him mad, but the pressure on my chest threatened to crack my ribcage. It took everything in me just to gasp in drops of air.

"I will not be left behind," he said, hushed. Much quieter than before. No longer giving his doomed sermon. But, despite its lower volume, it was filled with a determination that surpassed everything else he had said. It suggested to me that, despite his words, he did not care about salvation for mankind. He cared about salvation for himself. And he would destroy the world to get it.

He clicked his fingers and I dropped to the ground, landing on my hands and knees. I tried to stand, but another force held my hands to the ground.

"I will not kill you," Digby said, looking down at me. "A final favour for Rachel and Fred."

He turned his back on me. I gritted my teeth, but was still catching my breath, unable to yell at him.

He stopped by the demon.

"I cannot allow her to live, however. And I seem to be unable to trust you to finish the job. The imps will do it. They will also serve to destroy this place."

He paused and looked around. I saw no hint of sadness in his eyes.

"An end of an era," he said. "The start of another."

Digby proceeded down the aisle, his hands clasped behind his back. The demon looked at me, and then shook his head. Was that shame? Disappointment? Did it matter?

I heard the growls the moment the doors closed behind Digby and the archdemon. Hisses and flaming sputters filled the gaps between growls and deep chittering.

"Kat? Are you hurt?"

"I'm fine, Treth. But not sure for how long."

"Is his magic still holding?"

"Yes."

"Can you dispel it?"

"I'm not a wizard."

"Your demanzite?"

"I need hands to get it."

I felt fear wash over me. I felt a pang of appreciation for Treth's concern. At least he was afraid for my death. I was too busy pondering what I'd just learnt.

Digby, my childhood priest, was the ringleader. He was abducting the mages. He had ordered Cornelius and the demon to kill me. And he was insane.

Before I could ponder anymore, the stained glass exploded inwards, sending multi-coloured shards across the room. Red and black horned creatures poured into the church, their clawed hands afire. They tore towards me, while my hands were glued to the ground. If only I had one hand free. I could at least take a few of them down with me.

The pews, tapestries and carpets were ignited as the imps crossed them, barrelling across the room towards me.

"Kat…" Treth began.

"No need," I whispered. "I understand."

Treth smiled, sadly.

The imps were metres away. I felt the demonic heat swelter off their unnatural mottled flesh. Their horns did not look like any animal horns or those of the archdemon.

319

They were twisted. Unnatural. I could hear the hiss of steam as the imps' saliva hit the ground and evaporated from their own heat.

I didn't close my eyes. I'd stare death down, the way I'd done almost every single time before.

They were a metre away.

An imp licked its lips, revealing rows of jagged, razor teeth in a mouth as wide as its head.

They were so close. I felt like I was in an oven. If they didn't kill me, the heat would.

I still didn't close my eyes. I stared them down. Stared right into their yellow-red toxic eyes.

At least I'd heard the birds chirp one last time.

Cold replaced heat so suddenly that I felt nauseous. A wave of frost flooded the room, blanketing everything in a layer of bluish-white. Everything except me. The imps before me were frozen solid, their expressions looked comical in their icy state. Icicles hung from their horns.

Pranish? Was my first thought. But then I smelled rot. An all too familiar smell.

Zombies advanced towards me. No, not zombies. They were too coordinated. They moved like humans, despite their peeling, pale skin, and hollow eyes.

Flesh-puppets. Coordinated undead minions, directly under control by a necromancer or their lieutenants.

They moved into the room bearing sledgehammers, axes and even a shotgun, and proceeded to break the imps' frozen bodies. Only a single undead did not partake in the exercise. The undead man wore polished plate-mail, with a purple cape. Atop his head was a cavalier hat, bearing a purple plume. A thin blade was sheathed by his side.

He advanced towards me, and I felt myself unconsciously struggling to break my magical bonds.

Closer, I saw how old and preserved he was. Dry, blackened. Gaunt. Skin clinging to the bone. Hollow eyes, bearing a blue fire that spoke of a far-reaching intelligence. A wight. An intelligent undead.

"Kat...Drummond..." It rasped, shaky, as a mouth, long dead, created words it should have not been able to utter.

I stared, wide-eyed. I must admit, I felt fear now. They were my prey – the undead – but they were still my most extreme fear. I hated them above all else.

It clicked its fingers and I felt the pressure on my hands release. I stood, backing up towards the Virgin Mary.

"My mistress sends a message, Kat Drummond..." It trailed off at my name, cocked its head and continued. "You are not meant to die. Not yet."

At that, the wight turned and left. Its flesh puppet forces followed after, leaving the frozen imps in pieces.

I did not move, until long after the undead disappeared.

Chapter 21. The Trail

"I don't like it, Kat," Treth said.

"Me neither. But it isn't like I asked to be saved by the undead," I replied, only just catching my breath after our ordeal. My hands shook.

"Being helped by evil…it stinks of being evil. Are we on the right path?" Treth asked.

"Too far down it to look back now."

I was running. I'm not sure where. Just away from the frozen church, with its destroyed stained-glass windows and its stink of demons and undeath.

"What's the next move?" Treth asked, still a hint of reluctance in his voice. He hated the undead just as much as I did. If not more.

"We will figure out who this *mistress* is and what she wants with me after we're done. Digby is still out there, and so are the missing Titan Mages."

I clenched my fists as I ran. Digby had tried to kill me. He'd ordered Cornelius to kill me. He'd made me kill him.

This was personal.

"What is it he wants?" Treth asked.

I slowed down to catch my breath. The sky was darkening with rain clouds. Rare this time of the year.

"To destroy the world – or at least to cause enough damage that his vague prophecies come true."

"And how is he going to do that?"

"He's stealing mages. I suspect to use them as batteries to help him summon demons. That will be the adversary he needs for his holy war."

"He'd need an army of mages to summon the number of demons needed to destroy the world."

"No, not an army. He only needs enough to disrupt the Citadel. Cause if the mages stop their work…"

"The Titan awakes."

"And then we'd be left wishing it was just demons."

I stopped and looked around. I was…somewhere. I checked my cell phone. Thankfully, the demon hadn't fried it this time.

"We need to find out where he could have gone."

And then kill him. I'd resigned myself to that fact. I'd already killed Cornelius and Digby deserved to be killed far more than he had.

"Perhaps, phone the Citadel," Treth suggested. "They may have some way of tracking the mages."

"Why wouldn't they have used it already?"

"They thought the mages were dead…"

"Fair enough."

I dialled Charlotte.

"Ms Drummond? I am very busy. Has there been a problem with payment?"

"I know who took the mages."

Silence. I had her attention.

"Do you have any way to track them?" I asked.

"No," she said. "We would have tried already if we did. Who took them?"

"A priest. A Father Digby."

I almost spat the words.

"Digby, you say?"

She pondered the name.

"There was a Digby who worked for the Citadel years ago, when I was an intern. A Joshua Digby, I think."

Now, that was a shock.

"Yeah, I'm pretty sure there was a Joshua Digby. A sorcerer tasked with providing energy to the circle."

I heard the clatter of a keyboard.

"Here it is…" A pause. "He was fired. Considered a security risk. And you say he is the culprit?"

"Yes, he just tried to kill me - again."

"Congratulations on him not succeeding," Charlotte replied, drily.

"Do you have any idea where he might be hiding? Any records of his properties. His residences?"

"Our records are not that extensive. I'm sorry, Ms Drummond, but the meister needs something. Good luck with the search."

She hung up.

Good luck? I was trying to save her mages!

"So, Digby had history with the Citadel," I said, still holding my cell.

"Makes sense," Treth replied. "His crusade can't just be idealistic. There's a personal hate in his actions. There are a hundred ways to wreak destruction, but he chooses to harm those who wronged him before."

"So much for salvation."

"Humans are complex. Can have many concurrent reasons for doing one thing."

"You say humans like you aren't one."

"I'm not – anymore."

"You looked human to me."

Treth paused and didn't reply.

I needed to get home. To replenish my supplies. To repair and replace the armour that was damaged during my fight with the demon nights before. I was still dressed in the clothes, washed by the hospital, that I'd been wearing that night.

I called a taxi. On the drive, I thought about how I would track Digby down before he tried to kill me again or succeeded in his plan.

Charlotte didn't have his records. But that didn't mean no one did. Hope City was a bureaucratic quagmire. A quagmire that may contain the information I needed.

I hated the City Council. I hated governments in general. But I also knew I had a job to do. And if that meant making a deal with something worse than the devil, then so be it.

I phoned Trudie.

"Hey, Kats," Trudie said, cheerfully. I heard chatter and the clinking of mugs in the background. A café, by the sound of it.

"Is Andy with you?"

Hesitance. "Yes, why?"

"I need something from him. Something urgent."

A longer pause.

"Does this mean you're gonna stop being stupid?"

Stupid? I wasn't being stupid!

"Yes. But I need the help now. A lot of people are in danger. Can you ask Andy to pull some strings with his dad? I need a list of properties owned or connected to a Catholic priest named Joshua Digby."

"Your parents' old priest? Why? Actually, don't tell me."

I heard her speak, muffled, holding the phone to her chest as she spoke to Andy.

"He says he'll get the info to you within half an hour."

I was about to hang up.

"And Kat…make sure you actually forgive him after this."

"I will. Please say thank you on my behalf."

"You can do it yourself on campus!"

I hung up.

***

I was pacing my apartment, much to the distress of both Duer and Alex, when I felt the buzz of my cell. I drew it as fast as I would my sword. It had taken Andy longer than he'd said to get the details. Hours. It was fast approaching dusk, and I had already gone over my gear a hundred times.

It was Trudie's number, but an official looking digital document. A list of addresses connected to Digby, but none registered as his official residence. One address stood out. A property that anyone would find a parish priest owning peculiar. A property near Chapman's Peak, an expensive nature reserve on the coast of Hope City.

I sent another thank you in response and phoned Conrad. I'd need the lift, but knew I had to do this alone. Backup wouldn't help me against the demon. Only my slim hope that the demon would again refuse to kill me gave me some measure of comfort.

Hope, or no hope, I had no choice. Digby had tried to kill me. I'd return the favour. I was fair, if nothing else.

Chapter 22. Showdown

"My demon-fighting days are over," Conrad said, pulling up his handbreak. We were stopped below Chapman's Peak, parked by the once often used road. These days, people preferred the safer roads down South-East way. Rockfalls and the djinns that caused them made Chapman's Peak a scenic, but deadly route.

"Good. I need to do this alone," I said. My coat seemed to warm at my response. It glowed, faintly.

"Cindy?" Conrad offered.

I shook my head. "*She's* not even a match for this demon. And it would take too long to rally enough purifiers. I have a feeling Digby wants to end this tonight. I need to do it now, and by myself."

Conrad inclined his head with respect.

"I'll add a photo of you to my wall."

I snorted. "I'm not dead yet."

He grinned. "Just in case."

I unbuckled my seatbelt and got out.

"Hey, Kat," Conrad called, leaning outside his window. I stopped and looked at him.

"You're a good hunter."

I nodded and turned back to the cliff. It was the nicest thing Conrad had ever said to me.

The entrance to Digby's mountainside property was guarded by an old wire-mesh gate, rusting at the edges. I scaled it easily enough but felt the echo of an ache from my new flesh and recently knitted bone.

"Quietly," Treth reminded me.

I rolled my eyes. He really didn't need to do that. I'd been doing this for a long time now. Yet, I still smiled afterwards, if just at the reminder that he was still there.

The gate gave way to a dusty concrete stairway, with fresh foot-tracks. A single pair.

"Our demon friend doesn't leave tracks," Treth said.

"Friend, now?"

"Ssshhh. Sneak mode."

Yeah, yeah, I thought to myself, and scaled the stairs. It had a multitude of turns, twisting up the mountain, until finally reaching what looked to be a construction yard, jutting out of a cliff. Half of the attempt at a mountain villa, overlooking the Atlantic, was outside of the cliff, while the other half must have been carved out of the mountain itself.

331

Digby must have had some money. *How*, was a question for another time.

I arrived at the top of the staircase, staying low and watching the windowless holes in the building for lookouts. Demonic or otherwise. I saw nothing. Just the faint outlines of shovels, abandoned bricks and support beams.

I darted across the opening from the top of the staircase to the side of the under-construction villa and rested my back up against the wall. I listened.

The sound of the waves in the distance. The bellow of a ship horn. Seagulls. And, faintly, a voice.

I drew my wakizashi in my right hand and Voidshot in my left. Hopefully, my training with Brett would be enough to fire with my off-hand. It had been enough against Cornelius, at least.

I rounded the building until I found an entrance, and entered the darkness, my coat emitting a faint glow that soon died as I wished it to be so. This coat was becoming more and more useful.

The voice grew louder and clearer as I pressed further through the unfinished building. Abandoned construction gear was left on tarps and by support struts. I was careful not to knock anything over but was struggling to see as the concrete blocked the setting sun.

The building ceased at the rock of the cliff-face, where excavation had stopped, all except for a tunnel, leading down and lit with a string of fluorescent lights.

I kept Voidshot steady and my blade in a defensive stance as I descended. The voice grew louder. Digby. He was shouting at someone at great length about something, but I couldn't be sure who or what about.

I went further into the mountain.

"Kat!" Treth warned me. He didn't need to. I smelled the charred flesh of the imp before I saw it. I darted behind the wall, keeping myself as flat as possible, as the demon walked past. It was considering something stuck on its claw and did not notice me. I resisted breathing a sigh of relief as the demon passed and I proceeded, going the way it had come.

There were no doors in the cave complex, but a lot of empty rooms. Some had tarp, unopen paint cans and tools. Was Digby building something? How could he afford all of this? It was like a real evil lair from some old *James Bond* film.

I heard Digby's voice again, as I considered the freshly placed tiling of a side-room. I could hear him more clearly now.

"I need to proceed now…"

A pause. I didn't hear another voice. A phone call.

"No. The mission is almost blown. The Citadel must know about my plans now. They'll be searching for the mages."

Another pause.

"No!" he yelled, outraged. "I've come too far for this to be shut down. I need this. We need this! Salvation will come."

He stopped and didn't speak again. He, or the other person, must have hung up.

I approached closer to where the voice had come from, dodging a few imps as they patrolled. They looked irritable. No demon liked being enslaved to a mortal. It took a lot of power and duress to keep them shackled. Imps, I had read, were mischievous and malicious. Chaotic evil, if you were to simplify their nature. Having them patrolling a subterranean hallway was not their ideal job.

I rounded a corner and saw a glimpse of natural light. I peeked, and saw the back of Digby, a silhouette looking out onto the setting sun. He had carved this section of the cave overlooking the bay, out onto the dark Atlantic and the setting sun to the west. Two large red demons stood at a distance, flanking the priest. They had goat legs and massive upper bodies, topped by a large jawed head with horns as long as my swords. They carried two-handed blades, currently resting on their shoulders. From the sketches in the demonology books I'd read, they looked like hell spawn. Brutish demons theorised to be constructed from the essence of warfare.

The archdemon himself leant up against a pillar. His black suit was still impeccable. He was hiding his wings again. He let out an exaggerated yawn and began analysing his nails.

Treth did not dare speak. We still couldn't be sure what the archdemon wanted. He hadn't killed me yet, but that didn't mean he wouldn't help Digby kill me now. He was his servant, after all.

To the sides of the lair, I saw two doorways. A faint hum emanated from each. I saw a pale green glow. That type of magical evil green. I'd put money on it that the captured mages were being held captive there. And I'm not the gambling type.

I bit my lip. Only one angle of attack. Digby's back exposed. Ambush. Two guards. Magic. A third-force — the archdemon — who could destroy me instantly.

Maybe, I was the gambling type. And I was doubling-down on a terrible hand.

I checked Voidshot in my left-hand and swapped it with the blade. I needed to be sharp here. I was ambidextrous, but still favoured my right-hand.

I closed my eyes to focus. Took a quiet breath. Opened my eyes with a new clarity and rounded the corner. The sights lined up. My finger was on the trigger. The hell spawn hadn't reacted. I pulled the trigger. The bang rang out, causing a harsh ringing in my ears.

Digby didn't fall. He stood, facing outwards, his hands still clasped behind his back. The bullet hovered an inch from his head. He turned, got out of the way, and clicked his fingers. The bullet shot out towards the sea.

I tried to fire again, but the same force he used before knocked my gun out of my hand. I let the pistol hang loose by my side, still connected to my belt by its silver chain, as I attempted to charge in. Digby let me, before gesturing to the side of the room, sending me spiralling towards the wall.

What did I think would happen? That I'd somehow get the jump on him? That I could kill a sorcerer in his own lair?

Stupid.

"So, the imps failed?" Digby asked rhetorically. "Did someone help you?"

I didn't respond, even so he only held my arms to the wall.

"No matter. I'll be here now to ensure you die."

I felt a pressure on my throat. An immense force. It wasn't like someone strangling me. It was as if someone was slowly pressing a brick onto my throat. I couldn't breathe. I couldn't think. I felt Treth's fear. His feeling of shame and impotence at being unable to do anything to help me.

The pressure stopped.

"Actually…no."

Digby turned to the archdemon, who looked bored, leaning up against the wall. The hell spawn eyed me, blankly. They were awaiting explicit orders. Reluctant guards.

"I summoned you, monster. It is time you fulfil your mission. Kill the hunter," Digby commanded.

The archdemon looked at me, impassively. No smirk. No sadness.

He looked back at Digby. "No."

"Excuse me?"

The demon shrugged.

Digby let go of me as he turned his full force on the demon, lifting the creature up and towards the edge of the cliff. The demon hung limply as Digby held him out over the edge. I didn't know if Digby meant to scare him. A winged demon wasn't afraid of heights, much less this one.

"You are my servant, demon! You obey me."

The demon didn't respond. I used the opportunity to reach into my pocket and retrieve a sachet of demanzite. Its sandy shards scraped my flesh as Digby turned towards me and sent a wave of force, knocking me back into the wall, and the demanzite all over the floor. He held me there.

"If you won't do it, demon. I will."

He looked straight at me and held his hand out. I felt a new pain. On my chest. My heart. He was squeezing it.

I held my chest and tried to cry out. I couldn't.

Tears welled up.

My eyes glazed over.

I felt my organs flag. My arteries clog.

For another time, in such a short time, I was sure I was about to die.

But I was wrong then. And I was wrong now.

The pain stopped.

My vision returned and I saw Digby, facing me, with a hand through his chest. The demon's hand had impaled him from behind. Even then, no blood had stained his skin or suit. Immaculate, even after such bloody work.

The hell spawn disappeared in a burst of flame as the archdemon lifted Digby up, his head lolling, and dropped him into the sea. I heard the splatter as he hit the rockface on the way, and then the splash as he hit the water.

The demon looked at me, grinned his perfect white teeth, and disappeared.

Chapter 23. Pride

The Titan mages were alive and well. That is if 'well' was being comatose for weeks, hooked up to a combination of mundane and magical life support. It wasn't my idea of fun to spend weeks in a tank of green magic goo, but at least they hadn't been conscious for it. Their malnutrition and spark burnout weren't too severe. Nothing a bout of healing magic and good eating couldn't remedy.

As I had suspected, the mages were being used to power Digby's demonic summoning. Digby had only had enough power to summon the archdemon himself. An impressive feat all the same. Usually, sorcerers wouldn't risk sacrificing their spark to summon demons. Demon summoning was the domain of wizards, who drew their power from the weylines. Digby had spark to spare, however. Not enough, though, as the archdemon had wrestled out of his control and killed him in the end.

The Citadel gave me an extra reward for saving the mages. Including, a life-time pass up the mountain. It was a privilege normally reserved only for the upper echelons of the Titan Cult and Citadel. I'd be sure to use it, despite my bad memories of the place. Table Mountain was that nice a mountain I could forget that it entombed a primordial titan. At least for a little while.

Conrad took me to the healing clinic after my ordeal. I was apparently as pale as a phantom. I slept in the car. I didn't remember getting into bed.

I caught up on the lectures I missed during my absence in the following days. I did some more mundane, and safer, hunts. I looked into the Necrolord and pondered the wight who had saved me, and his mistress. But, info was sparse, and I could not find anything more on my mysterious saviours. I didn't even want to think of them as that.

Colin asked me on another date. A movie. While I was still confused over what I really wanted, I knew that I liked Colin. That was more than I could say about most things. While the sci-fi feature film played in the background, I made sure that my hand met his, and couldn't help but feel satisfaction emanate from Treth, watching over my shoulder.

I made amends with Andy. He had pulled through in the end. I didn't really trust him, still. There was just something off about him, but I was fine with him dating my best friend now. Without him, I wouldn't have been able to find Digby, after all.

It was after a lunch with Trudie, Pranish and Andy that I left campus once again feeling that comfortable monotony of university life. It was also then that I reached into my pocket and found a note.

It was written in fine cursive and smelled like tobacco.

"The rock. On the mountain. For questions left unanswered."

I crumpled the note in one hand and shoved it back into my pocket.

***

My pass let me up the cable car. There were only new faces at the Whiteshield guard post and manning the cars. They looked young. None looked arrogant. They knew what had happened to those who came before them. Bloodstains on the asphalt remained as a sobering reminder.

It had been a while since I had been on top of the mountain. It was windy and smelled like fynbos. I recalled being here at night and shivered. It was much more pleasant during the day.

The black suited demon was where he said I'd find him. He was standing. Looking out over the city, his hands clasped behind his back, facing away. His horns were shorter than I remembered them, only just peaking out above his medium length, wavy black hair.

I approached hesitantly, feeling Treth's worry. I was sure, however, that if the demon wanted me dead, I'd be dead.

"It's a beautiful city," he said, before I could speak.

I looked out. It was nice, but the smog from the slums wasn't a pleasant sight.

"Even the slums," he said, as if reading my mind. "Sure, you see them as a rot. And perhaps, they are. But in that rot, among the festering corruption, there are still people. People striving. People living. People doing something…"

He took a deep breath.

"Existence is suffering, Digby said, but it is so much more. It is a perseverance that I so enjoy watching. To observe life, in all its interesting forms. Poverty, prosperity, peace, love and war. It is all a product of the same thing. And all so…fascinating."

He trailed off. Silence.

"Why did you kill Digby?" I finally asked, breaking the silence.

He spoke without turning. I approached closer, not knowing why. He smelled like pipe tobacco and *Old Spice*. He must have started smoking again.

"Because I could. Because I'd grown bored of him. Because he tried to harm me. Because he disrespected me."

He paused. "Or because I'd decided that it was time to end the charade."

"You were never really his servant, were you?"

He looked at me, a hint of a smirk on his lips, and then turned back to the city.

"Why didn't you kill me?" I asked.

A gust of wind caught my coat. It did nothing to his hair or suit.

"There was nothing to be proud of in victory over you. I delight in a challenge. A fight with you, a mortal, was not fair."

"Well, thanks for the affirmation."

He turned towards me, and his expression was stern.

"Do not misunderstand me, hunter. You are greater than most of your kind. A broken soul...perhaps, no longer. Broken once but forged anew. Stronger, this time. But as strong as it can get, you will never be able to defeat me."

He looked away.

"No one can."

The question had been on the tip of my tongue for a while, but finally, I asked it.

"Who...who are you?"

He smiled, showing a row of white teeth.

"A wonderful question. One with many answers. One that could easily be answered with a word. A name. But a name is such a powerful thing. Yet so weak. With it, you can control. You can destroy. It is our greatest vulnerability. But...it is also the source of our pride. We want the ages to know our name. To know of our existence. We want to etch our names onto eternity. For all to see. Yet, if we do so, we risk everything."

He stared out for a few seconds. "But that is what makes it so interesting a thing. Something to be proud of. For something is only worth it if you can lose it. And the greatest folly only comes from the greatest accomplishments."

We gazed out over the city for moments more. Moments turned to minutes. The sun shifted its position across the blue sky.

"Digby was not the only one," the demon finally said. "There are others moving in the dark. You heard him speak to them before his death."

"What do they want?"

"To play God." He shrugged. "To shape reality to their whims. What else do we all want?"

I glared at him, only thinly realising the danger of that. He only laughed.

"That expression. That is why I didn't kill you."

His stern expression returned.

"The enemies in the shadows are numerous. Even I do not know the extent of their reach. Step carefully. Digby may have failed to awaken Adamastor to achieve his religious fantasies, but there are others who are much smarter and more capable. They are coming."

"I'll stop them."

The demon stared at me, impassive, before a grin lit up his face.

"I'm sure you will."

He walked forward, towards the edge. I did not move.

"That is all I can answer."

"Can, or will?"

He turned, with a mischievous smile.

"I don't lie."

"Just what a liar would say."

He laughed.

"Goodbye, Katherine Marigold Drummond. Until we meet again."

He disappeared. Treth and I did not speak for a while after. We observed Hope City, stretching out into the horizon. Our city. Our home.

"Was he evil?" I asked, finally, to Treth and to myself.

"I think he was more than evil," Treth said. "A force that predates evil."

"Is that even possible?"

"I don't know. You're the philosopher type."

"I'm an historian."

"Little difference where I'm from."

I smiled, faintly. For the first time in a long time, it was a truly happy smile.

"Let's go home, Treth."

Afterword

As of writing this, this book is probably my favourite of Kat's adventures. The most notable reason for this is probably that this story allowed me to explore not only some more emotionally intense parts of Kat's backstory, but also some of her philosophy, beliefs views on morality.

Kat is a complicated character. Yes, she's snarky and a bad-ass (two essential characteristics!) but she also has an intense melancholy about her, stemming from her background. This story, I feel helped to illustrate something implied in previous books, but not explored too much. Kat's intelligence.

The archdemon in this book is by far my favourite of Kat's (not so adversarial) adversaries. As a writer, I felt he provided a great foil for Kat to figure out her own beliefs and argue them.

And for those reasons, and others, I loved writing this book, and I hope you loved reading it!

Acknowledgements

While books are (often) the work of a single person, they take a veritable organisation to produce. I'm an independent author because I value my freedom and am sceptical of the traditional publishing industry. While this makes some aspects of my business easier, it also means that I lack a certain connection to an institution. Succinctly: this is a lonely career.

But there are people in my life who have helped me along and have been integral to the creation of this book and series.

It takes a lot of patience to write six books before releasing a single one, and without the feedback and conversation of my beta reader, Chelsea Murphy, I would have gone insane a long time ago. Thank you!

I would also like to thank my mother for providing her editing skills to get these books into a condition fit for human consumption, and for being someone I can always natter to about Kat, Hope City and necromancy.

Thank you to Deranged Doctor Design for the wonderful cover art. I advise them to any author looking for a professional design.

And finally: thank you. Without you, this book would not be read and enjoyed. Without you, these words are just the scribblings of a half-mad author.

So, thank you!

And until next time.

Nicholas Woode-Smith is a full-time fantasy and science fiction author from Cape Town, South Africa. He has a degree in philosophy and economic history from the University of Cape Town. In his off-time, he plays PC strategy games, Magic: The Gathering, and Dungeons & Dragons.

Follow him on Facebook:

https://www.facebook.com/nickwoodesmith/

Made in the USA
Middletown, DE
27 March 2021